KENTON'S
VINTAGE AFFAIR

JANICE L. DENNIE

KENTE ROMANCE
An Imprint of Kente Publications
P.O. Box 184
Jackson, CA 95642

Copyright © 2014 Janice L. Dennie
ISBN-10: 0964334933
ISBN-13: 9780964334939

DEDICATION

This book is dedicated to Gregory D. Reed Sr., my husband, and best friend. My cousin Adwoa Dunn-Mouton, who introduced me to Low Country cuisine. My earthly father Lawrence H. Dennie Sr., who read bedtime stories to me when I was a child. My mother Wilma J. Jackson-Dennie, who taught me to love all genres of literature. To my heavenly father.

THE UNDERWOOD FAMILY

Frank Underwood & Henrietta Underwood
Children:
-Joseph Underwood

Joseph Underwood & Jewell Underwood
Children:
-Kenton Underwood
-Justin Underwood
-Carter Underwood
-Brandon Underwood
-Crystal Underwood

Joshua Underwood & Eunice Underwood
Children:
-Daniel Underwood
-Delores Underwood

Frank and Joshua are brothers.

Daniel Underwood & Angela Underwood
Children:
-Tisha Underwood
-Jason Underwood

You can enjoy this book as a standalone or read it as part of the series.

Dear Reader,

I've always loved visiting Napa Valley with its bucolic landscape and fine dining. I decided to write this book when I became aware of the presence of African American wineries, in the Valley. Three vintners participated in a private wine tasting and panel discussion that my chapter of a non-profit organization hosted. The panel discussion was enlightening; the wines unforgettable.

Some past, and present African American wineries, located within Napa Valley, and throughout the State of California have been listed in the back of this book.

In Kenton's Vintage Affair, Briana Rutledge is an independent, yet vulnerable, woman who wants to open her dream restaurant. Fire ignites, when she inherits a cottage next door to handsome vintner, Kenton Underwood, the eldest of the Underwood brothers.

Sit back, relax and enjoy reading "Kenton's Vintage Affair."

Janice

Chapter 1

Briana Rutledge stood in the cold morning fog gazing at a dilapidated wooden cottage. She'd recently inherited the cottage from her grandmother who raised her mother there. She hoped to find something inside to bring closure to many years of missing a mother she'd never known.

Walking up the rickety steps, she wondered how many times her mother had played on them as a child. She tried to look inside through the cloudy picture window, but decades of caked on dirt and hard rain blocked her view. She twisted her rusty key in the brass doorknob, but it wouldn't move. Holding the key with both hands, she twisted it again with all of her strength, and then it broke off. Not one for giving up without a fight, she walked around the cottage to try the back door.

She twisted the back door knob, but it wouldn't open. She pushed it hard with her shoulder, and it still wouldn't open. She kicked in the bottom and then the soft wood easily yielded. By pushing the top of the door with her shoulder and kicking the bottom, it finally busted off the hinges crashing onto the floor, Briana falling with it. Bracing herself for the fall, Briana found herself sitting on top of the door coughing and waving her hands to clear thick dust flying through the air. Closing her eyes, she covered her nose with her jacket collar so she could breathe. "Whew," she huffed. "That was no easy task."

Kenton Underwood combed through his vineyard inspecting the underside of some cabernet leaves for diseases. His family's five thousand acre Tuscan style winery bordered by country villas and large estate wineries sat high on a hill, above the vineyard making a picturesque backdrop for Kenton to work. As he reached the edge of his vineyard, a movement caught his eye, prompting him to look up.

A woman stood on the porch of the old shack next door trying to get inside. She couldn't be a burglar, because she was too well dressed in her yellow leather jacket, black boots and black skinny jeans. Why was she trying to get inside? He knew the property wasn't for sale, because he tried to purchase it years ago.

Kenton had a natural tendency to protect his environment and family, so when the woman walked down the side of the cottage he decided to investigate. Brushing the dirt off of his hands and slapping the dirt off of his jeans, he mounted his work horse and rode across the open field next to the shack.

Startled, and shaken from her fall, and still sitting on the door rubbing her sore arm, Briana looked forward and saw a pair of muddy cowboy boots in the open doorway. Her eyes moved upward and met the handsome gaze of a six foot two, dark brown, sexy young man, sharply assessing her under thick dark brows drawn into a frown. The shadow on his unshaven chiseled jaw gave him a masculine look along with his coal black hair and mustache. She could tell his shoulders were wide underneath his jean jacket and plain white t-shirt. His strong thighs filled out his faded blue jeans, and his long legs seemed to go on forever. She'd never seen a more handsome man than this stranger. "Who are you?" she asked.

Kenton watched the woman; his gaze cool. "Who are you?" He stared at the thin coat of dust covering the woman. Thick particles of microscopic debris flew all around her body. His first instinct was to help her up, but he knew she hadn't fallen by accident, because he saw her trying to enter through the front door. He almost bent his knees to help her up, but then straightened back up and crossed his arms across his chest. Before helping her up, he needed to know who she was, and why she was inside the shack. He doubted that she owned the property because he'd known for all of his twenty-nine years that his grandmother's good friend owned the cottage and lived out of town.

"I was…I own this cottage." Briana's mouth was dry. She had a tendency to stutter and drawl whenever she was nervous.

He looked at her, but she looked away. He concluded she was lying. "No one's lived here for years." He reached for his cell phone.

"What are you doing?" Briana asked.

"I'm calling the police," he said, dialing 911.

"Wait!" Briana said. "I'm a guest of Henrietta Underwood. She lives next door. She knows I own this property. You can ask her if you don't believe me."

He relaxed at the mention of his grandmother's name. He ended the call and placed the phone back in its case. He walked into the room and held out his hand, a grin crossing his face. "Name's Kenton Underwood. I'm Henrietta's grandson."

The tension melted from Briana's body. Henrietta mentioned last night that her grandson, Kenton was coming back today.

He took her hand and pulled her to her feet.

His touch sent a warm shiver up her arm. Once up, she straightened her clothing, brushed away tiny splinters of wood from her sleeve, and rubbed her aching arm.

Kenton watched her rub her arm. He hoped she wasn't hurt. It was kind of funny, for such a skinny woman to pack such a wallop knocking the door down. Smiling, he leaned his shoulder against the broken door frame running his index finger down a rusty hinge.

"I see you broke the door down."

"Ya think?"

With a trace of humor in his voice, he touched the sides of his face to replicate the dust on her face. "You have dust," he paused, "on your face and hair." He watched her as she wiped her face with the back of her hand.

Taking out a rag from his back pocket, he offered. "You can use this."

Jerking her head back, Briana gave him an offensive look. "Thank you, but no. I don't know where that rag has been."

He held her chin and wiped away the dust. "I assure you this rag is clean." He looked her over. "So, do you have a name?"

"My name is Briana Rutledge."

"Briana Rutledge," he murmured. Her soft drawl caught his attention. Where was she from?

"You must be the grandson who was visiting London?" Briana said, her sandy brown ponytail tickled her neck as she spoke.

"I am." He paused.

"Miss Henrietta told me all about you last night." Amusement flashed in her eyes, like rich lush green Spanish olives. "I flew in from Baton Rouge yesterday and spent the evening with your grandmother."

Kenton stroked his chin. "How do you know my grandmother?"

"Miss Henrietta was my grandmother's good friend. My grandmother owned this property."

"Mrs. Lillie Thomas from Baton Rouge owns this property. My grandmother has talked about her for years. She even mentioned that Lillie had a granddaughter. That must be you."

Briana nodded. "I've known Miss Henrietta all of my life. She wanted to attend my grandmother's funeral, but couldn't make it because she fell."

"That's right. She did fall a couple of months ago. " Kenton recalled the incident as if happened yesterday— he was the one who'd taken his grandmother to the hospital. "She mentioned wanting to attend a funeral in Baton Rouge." Kenton looked into Briana's eyes. "I'm sorry to hear about your grandmother."

Briana lowered her head. "Thank you." She looked back up and glanced around as if mentioning her grandmother brought too much pain. "Miss Henrietta invited me to stay with her after my grandmother's funeral. My grandparent's raised my mother here." She glanced at the laundry room near the back door then back to Kenton. "I'm going to take a look around. You're welcome to join me."

It took a few seconds for the invitation to register with Kenton. Although he had a lot of work to do in the vineyard today, he couldn't resist her invitation—he wanted to know more about this lovely creature. Anyway, work probably wasn't a good idea since jet lag was kicking in.

A dank whiff of mold assaulted Briana's nose as she went through the house. She opened windows as she walked around, to air out the place. Shivering in the cold, damp dwelling, she slid her hands into her coat pockets.

Their footsteps echoed throughout the small cottage as they walked. She liked the light oak wood floor. Everywhere she looked, she could see her grandmother's hand in the décor—right down to her grandmother's favorite color, green, covering every single wall. She saw an old country kitchen sink mounted below cabinets painted a faded pea green and accented with white plastic knobs.

Briana felt the decaying wooden floor cave in. She took a step back.

"It's dangerous in here." Kenton warned.

"I agree, but I have to look around."

"An inspector should check this place out before we go any farther."

"You're here with me. Why don't you check things out?"

"Okay. I'll lead the way."

"Thanks for the offer, but I can find my way around." With her next step, Briana felt her foot falling through a weakened plank. She turned her head. "Maybe I better let you lead the way."

"I thought so." At least the smart-mouthed, hard-headed woman had enough sense to let him lead the way.

Holding onto his shoulder for security, Briana followed behind him. Streams of light filtered into the dark rooms through torn shades guiding their footsteps as they toured the cottage. Her steps slowed down as she thought about her mother living in this tiny house. Having been raised by her grandparents at their Baton Rouge estate, Briana had no idea that her mother had lived so modestly.

As they moved around, paying close attention to the squeaky floor, Kenton asked, "Does this place have special meaning to you?"

"This is where my mother grew up." She hoped to find a key chain, a pencil or anything that had belonged to her mother.

They walked down the narrow hallway leading to the bedrooms. They reached the master bedroom wallpapered in a green floral print. "This must have been my grandparent's bedroom." She looked down the hall and pointed to the other small bedroom. "That room over there," her voice softened, "must have been my mother's room." The moment her touch was gone,

Kenton turned his head and watched her walk into the bedroom.

Standing in the hot pink bedroom, Briana felt nothing. She wandered over to the window and rolled up the cracked shade. She thought she would feel her mother's connection. Gazing through the window, Briana saw a huge Douglas fir tree that reminded her of Christmas.

Briana continued to walk around the bedroom running her fingers against the walls. After opening the closet door, she looked down on the pale oak floor and saw a faded drawing of a blue bird with a yellow beak drawn by a child. Picking up the drawing, she felt a warm current run from her fingertips up the length of her once aching arm. A sense of peace came over her body as she saw the name Ariana printed on the bottom in crooked letters with blue crayon. Ariana was her mother's name. For the first time in her life, she felt a warm connection with her mother. Now, she could feel her mother's love embracing her in this room, closing up the hollowness in her core. Bringing a shaky hand to her mouth, she leaned against the closet door frame. "No. I'm not going to cry," she said out loud. Although Briana hated for people to see her cry, uncontrollable tears made a path down her cheeks. She believed the bluebird drawing was a sign of her mother's love.

Minutes later, Kenton walked in on Briana standing by the closet door staring at a piece of paper with tears in her eyes. He walked up to her, and wiped away her tears with his thumbs.

"My mother grew up in this house." She exhaled slowly. "I've never been here before." She held the drawing close to her heart. "My mother stood right where I'm standing." With glistening eyes, she studied the room. "I can imagine her fighting, crying and laughing with my grandparents in this room." She turned the drawing around for him to see. "My mother's name was Ariana. She and my father died in a car crash when I was two years old. I never knew them."

An orphan. In that moment, Briana found a special place in Kenton's heart. He pictured himself in her situation. What if he'd never known his father? Where would he be?

Kenton inherited the character DNA of his male ancestors, a line of old fashioned southern gentlemen who took great pride in protecting their loved ones. His father taught him to respect women. Though his father referred to women as the weaker sex, Kenton didn't believe women were weak. His father had been a great influence on his life, but he'd never given much thought of how lucky he was until now. If it hadn't been for his father who had groomed him from a boy to take over the family business, he wouldn't be a successful vintner today.

"I'm sorry to hear about your parents," he said softly. He touched her elbow. "You okay?"

Briana nodded. "I'm fine."

Kenton wanted to hold her in his arms to ease her pain, but since they'd just met, he didn't think that would be appropriate.

"Would you mind giving me a moment alone?" She needed to collect herself. She could only imagine what he was thinking.

"No problem," he said. "I'll wait on the back porch."

On the porch, Kenton unbuttoned his jacket, noticing the morning fog had burned away. He leaned over and petted his horse that was tied to the bannister, but his thoughts were on the smart-mouthed, hard-headed young woman who'd just stolen his heart. He was captivated by her vulnerability. He wanted to get to know her better.

Briana wandered around the bedroom, savoring the emotional connection she'd made with her mother. Finding the drawing, a symbol of her mother's love, was more than she could have ever hoped. She'd accomplished what she came to do. With one last look, she turned and left the room, hugging her treasured artwork.

Chapter 2

Kenton sat on the porch steps waiting for Briana to come out. His face lit up when he turned around and saw her smiling at him. Rising in one fluid motion, he cleared his throat. "Feeling better?"

"Yes." She smiled. "Thank you for asking."

"How's your arm?"

"It doesn't hurt anymore," she said rubbing her healed arm.

"How about a tour of your land?"

"No, I don't think so. I wanted to have breakfast with Miss Henrietta."

"Breakfast?" Turning up his smile a notch, he looked at the time on his watch. "It's almost noon. "Why don't you join her for dinner instead?"

Briana looked out over rolling hills covered with green grass and giant oak trees. "I don't need a tour. I can see my property fine from here."

Shaking his head at this stubborn woman, he said. "You can't appreciate the beauty of your land from the back porch." He'd ridden through parts of her property many times in the past. "Your property has views that will take your breath away."

"Okay. Okay. I'm curious. Take my breath away." Briana grinned.

"The best views are by horseback." He nodded toward his horse. "You ride?"

"Do I ride?" She gave him a smug look, her grin growing wider. "Of course I ride. My grandfather taught me when I was eight." They walked through the tall weeds and wildflowers along the side of the house. Briana stood in front of her rental car.

"I'll ride old Gus here back to the stables." He pointed to the stables beside his vineyard. "Drive over to the stables. I'll meet you there."

Opening the door of her car, Briana placed her mother's drawing on the passenger seat. As she drove to the stables, she basked in the memories of how whole she'd felt standing in her mother's bedroom. Nothing could buy that feeling—nothing.

Kenton stood just inside of the stables when Briana arrived. She pulled her small satchel from the back seat, and slid the narrow strap across her chest, before exiting the car.

There were six stalls lined against the back wall. After they had passed several horses, they came to a stunning Strawberry Roan mare. Kenton took Briana's small hand into his. "Let me introduce you to your horse." He rubbed the mare gently on her face. "Briana, this is Beauty." He paused for a second. "Beauty, this is Briana."

"The name fits. She's beautiful." Looking into the horse's large brown eyes, Briana held her hand under Beauty's nose to introduce herself. The mare accepted Briana by smell and touch.

Kenton led Coal, his black stallion, out of his stall while Briana led Beauty out of hers. After saddling both horses, Kenton held a stirrup steady for Briana as she expertly mounted Beauty. He mounted Coal, and they rode across the grassy knolls to the trails peppered with large oak trees. They came to a breathtaking view of Napa Valley and stopped to admire the lush vineyards. Kenton pointed to the Napa River pouring into the Bay.

Glancing at Kenton, Briana saw how masculine he looked riding Coal. Sitting with an easy posture in his saddle, he reminded her of a cowboy straight out of an old Hollywood western. "So. How's the weather around here?"

An easy smile played at the corners of his mouth. "Cool in the mornings. Warm in the afternoon. Cool at night." The mid-day sun had warmed the air, so Kenton wiped a little perspiration from his brow. "Winters can get cold though. Sometimes down to twenty degrees."

Briana wanted to see the boundaries of her property. She decided to show him a description of her property lines from her deed. She'd made a copy of it before leaving Baton Rouge. She pulled the paper from her satchel and held it out to Kenton.

"Why are you showing me your deed?"

"I was hoping you could show me the property boundaries?"

"Okay, let's see." Kenton pointed toward the boundaries as he read.

"Wow. I didn't realize my land went out so far.

"Do you know the value of your land?"

"Not really. I didn't pay attention. My grandparents raised me with Black, southern working class values. They didn't raise me to be a pampered princess."

Kenton laughed. "You've got your values in the right place."

"I'm glad that my grandparents bought this property because it will help me achieve my goals."

She caught his attention. "Goals. What are your goals?"

Leaning back in her saddle, Briana looked out at the choppy grey-crested waves of the bay. "To accomplish something important in life."

Kenton was happy to hear that Briana wanted to accomplish something important. The more time he spent with Briana, the more he became intrigued with her.

Briana quietly rode along in her saddle. To break the silence, she began talking about Kenton's grandmother.

"Miss Henrietta reminds me of my grandmother with her easy going ways. She wasn't a big city dweller. I guess I'm not a big city dweller either. I prefer living a relaxed country lifestyle."

Turning his head, Kenton looked at Briana. "I enjoy living a relaxed country lifestyle too." Kenton saw Briana fidgeting in her saddle. "I can tell you're getting uncomfortable." He decided to take a short break to show her his ranch down the trail. "How about riding around one acre of your property today? We can see the rest of it another time."

Briana rubbed her bottom. "Thanks."

Later when they reached his ranch. Briana was impressed with the beauty of the property. "I see you have five horses." She watched one horse drink from a creek running through the middle of the corral. A young red headed man with freckles walked out of the barn pushing a wheel barrel full of hay.

"Who's that?"

"That's Tom. He's a deaf-mute. He gets room and board in exchange for feeding and grooming the horses." Kenton dismounted the horse, stretched, his legs and said. "I love this ranch, but I'm never here." He looked up at Briana put his hands around her waist to help her down.

Briana smiled. "So where did you get the horses?"

"They're rescue horses."

"Rescued from what?"

"Abandonment. Starvation." He paused for a second. "When ranchers can't afford to feed them, I take care of them."

Briana admired Kenton's compassion. "I'm glad you save horses."

They shared a smile. "When I come here I look forward to the peace." His ranch had everything, except a woman's touch. "Want to see inside?"

"I'll do anything to take a break from riding." Briana looked past him at the two-story redwood home. A creek bubbled its way down the hill. Briana marveled at the door at least eight feet high. She looked up at the vaulted ceiling supported by rough-hewn beams. All the floors were dark hardwood. Overstuffed chocolate leather furniture filled the living room. A gorgeous Elizabeth Catlett sculpture of a Native American woman placed on a rustic table caught Briana's eye. A dream catcher hung above the stone fireplace, and a huge Navajo rug took center stage in the center of the room.

"This is a fantastic house."

"Thank you, but it lacks a woman's touch."

Briana walked into the master bedroom and stopped in her tracks. Floor to ceiling shelving inside his open closet held rows upon rows of cowboy boots.

"Seriously?" Briana turned to Kenton.

Kenton threw back his head and laughed. "I collect them. I confess, it's my vice."

"Your house is gorgeous, but what I'd like to see is the kitchen?"

He took her to the kitchen. "This is a kitchen after my own heart." Briana ran her hand over the marble counter. "Do you mind if I come over and cook sometime?"

Kenton walked up behind Briana and whispered. "You can cook in here...any...time...you want." He put emphasis on each word.

His breath was warm on the back of her neck. He was so close that if she turned around they would be face to face. His nearness made her senses spin. She flattened up against the counter and slid away from him. "Oh, this is an interesting refrigerator."

"You don't want to know about the refrigerator?"

"No. I don't want to know about the refrigerator." She paused. "I want to know about the rug."

Kenton laughed. Briana grinned.

"I've got something else to show you before we go back."

They rode their horses until they reached the peak of a hill. Briana looked down at the field of orange flowers. "I've never seen anything like this."

"They're called poppies."

Briana looked around at the field of poppies. "I could be happy here."

He looked at her. "Does that mean you're going to stay?"

Kenton slid off his horse and knelt on one knee. He picked some flowers and held the bouquet up to Briana. "Poppies are California's state flower."

When they arrived at Henrietta's, Briana went straight to her room to rest. She sank into the plush chair beside her bed and closed her eyes. Today changed Briana. She thought about all of the wonderful things that went on in the cottage. Finding the drawing and making a connection with her mother that closed the hollowness in her core. Meeting and developing an attraction to Kenton. She'd seen the empathy, the compassion in his eyes. Both were good qualities in a husband. Husband? What was she thinking? Briana knew she wasn't looking for a husband. Ever. After what she'd been through. No way. When it came to love, Briana held a deep-seated secret. Her poppy field, not only took her breath away, but it made her feel happy and welcome to Napa. She knew without a doubt that she wanted to live here. She couldn't imagine walking away from all of the blessings she experienced today.

Chapter 3

Ruby Pitts, the family cook, was preparing dinner when Kenton and Briana arrived. As a senior member of First Avenue Baptist church in the neighboring city of Vallejo, the religious seventy-two-year-old woman put extra emphasis on saving every young person from their sins. Although Henrietta paid her well, Ruby spent most of her money on her drug addicted nephew. Born and raised in Oklahoma City, Ruby wore a tattered wig and no makeup. Due to a hearing problem, she spoke in a loud, flat monotone.

"Where's Granny, Ruby?" Kenton spoke loudly sticking his head through the door.

"She left a minute ago. Maybe she gettin' dressed for dinner. It should be ready 'bout thirty minutes." Ruby always said she prepared meals according to Henrietta's low-sodium, low-fat diet. She prepared bland meals because she wasn't a good cook. She'd worked in a laundry most of her life. She'd almost lost her house after taking out a loan for her nephew. That's when Henrietta hired Ruby as her cook and housekeeper, providing her good friend with a substantial raise.

Kenton walked up the grand staircase two steps at a time to the second floor. He knocked on Briana's door. "Briana, I'll come and get you for dinner in an hour."

The knock on the door broke Briana out of her daydream. "I'll be ready." Briana jumped out of the chair and ran into the bath.

Kenton entered his tan, ivory and chocolate bedroom. After removing his sweaty clothes, he stepped into the shower and lathered his body with a spicy scented soap. Warm beads of water slid from his face to his feet as images of Briana's olive green eyes lingered in his mind. A wide grin crossed his face as he recalled her response when they rode through that poppy field. He could still see how ethereal she looked. He asked himself, how a little flower could have such a strong effect on a woman like Briana.

He'd opened his heart to Briana after finding out she was an orphan. He didn't know why he felt this way about Briana all he knew was that he wanted to hold her, protect her, and ease her pain. He'd never felt that way about a woman before. He'd traveled around the world, and knew many young women, but not one touched his heart like Briana.

After showering, he pulled on his navy slacks, his thoughts were still on Briana. He felt lucky to have a beautiful woman, living in the house right down the hall from him. Walking to Briana's room, he knocked on her door.

"Yes."

"Are you ready?"

"Give me a minute. I'll be right out."

"I'll wait for you down the hall." He walked over to the window at the end of the hallway and stared into the vast openness of the rolling hills thinking of Briana. Minutes later he watched Briana walk down the hall wearing a long sleeve olive green, knee length wrap dress that accentuated her tiny waist. She accessorized her outfit with diamond studs and brown leather stilettos.

A slow smile built on Kenton's face as he scanned the beautiful, vulnerable woman walking down the hall in his direction. She cleaned up nicely; he thought. Only hours ago, she was covered with dust. When she reached him, Kenton locked eyes with Briana. His gaze fell from her smooth face to the creamy expanse of her neckline to the fullness of her breasts. "You look stunning Briana."

Briana's green eyes lightened at Kenton's compliment. "Thank you," she replied in a soft drawl. She loved hearing the way he pronounced her name, with his deep, sexy voice. "I have something to tell you Kenton, but promise not to tell your grandmother until I've had a chance to think it through."

"What's that?" Kenton asked taking a step closer, touching her hand softly.

Briana's body tingled at his touch. The heady scent of his spicy cologne, the sound of his sexy voice, and the confidence she saw in his eyes, made Briana aware that she was becoming attracted to Kenton. She glanced away from his gaze and continued her statement.

"I've decided to tear down my grandmother's cottage and turn it into a restaurant."

"A restaurant?" Kenton paused. "When did you decide that?"

"After we came back."

Kenton remained silent and let her do the talking.

"I'm going to name it Poppy Hill, after that beautiful poppy field. I can't get those flowers out of my mind."

Taking a step closer, he stroked his chin. "So let me get this right. You're going to open a restaurant, and you're going to name it Poppy Hill." He leaned against the window, wanting to pull her into his embrace. Able to think on his feet, he asked. "Have you ever owned a restaurant before?"

"I've worked as a chef in a five-star restaurant in New Orleans, and I love to cook."

Kenton quickly noticed that she evaded his question. He reserved his critical assessment of her answer for another time. For now, he focused on the positive. "A beautiful woman who loves to cook," He gave her an inquisitive look. "What kind of food are you going to serve in your restaurant?"

"Low Country. My grandmother taught me from a little girl how to prepare her famous recipes. Miss Henrietta loves my grandmother's mustard greens."

Kenton noticed that Briana wore no nail polish. Perhaps because she worked as a chef. He gave her a curious look. "Low Country," he paused. "What's that?"

"It is a healthy way of preparing soul food."

"So you're going to serve healthy soul food? That's different." Kenton loved soul food. He thought about the diverse population of Bay Area residents with its heavy Asian and Latino influence. "You know people from all over the world live in the Bay Area. We have a very diverse population. They will be your customers."

All anyone has to do is try my grandmother's recipes once. I guarantee they'll come back for more."

Kenton smiled thinking about his mother who never cooked a day in her life. His sister either. His grandmother used to cook soul food when he was younger, but now she was too frail. When he wanted some down home soul food, he drove to Oakland and ate at a popular restaurant in Jack London Square. He adored well-prepared home cooked meals.

"I'll prepare you and Miss Henrietta some of my grandmother's favorite recipes. I guarantee you will love my cooking."

"I can't wait." He rubbed his stomach. "So, you're going to name your restaurant, Poppy Hill?"

Smiling, Briana said, "Yeah."

"I'll keep your secret." Kenton led the way down the hall.

Descending the staircase side by side, they walked through the spacious living room that led into the elegant dining room, where they met Henrietta, the family matriarch, seated at the head of the table.

Henrietta Underwood was the daughter of sharecroppers, born at the beginning of the great depression. She was no stranger to poverty. Since her recent fall, she'd supported her substantial body by walking with a cane.

Henrietta scrutinized Kenton with great interest as she watched him rush over to pull out a chair for Briana. He, usually, sat at the foot of the table, but today he pulled out a chair across from Briana.

Henrietta's dream was to marry off all of her grandchildren before she died. Maybe her dream would come true with these two sitting next to her. Blessed with a warm, easy personality, Henrietta took Briana's hand in a gesture of love. "I see you've met my grandson."

Briana looked across the table at Kenton wearing a wide, mischievous grin on his face. "We met this morning in Nana's cottage."

Henrietta's smile broadened. "After you didn't join me for breakfast, I figured you went there to see the cottage."

Briana stood and kissed Henrietta. "I woke up at around five o'clock this morning, but I was too excited to sleep or eat, so I drove over to see Nana's cottage."

Amusement flickered in Henrietta's brown eyes. She was happy that Briana had come to visit, even though it was for a sad reason. Tucking a cloth napkin under the neckline of her blouse, Henrietta said to Kenton. "Briana flew in from Baton Rouge early last night. You've heard me talk about my friend Lillie in Louisiana."

Kenton nodded his head.

"Well, three weeks ago she died. Briana is Lillie's granddaughter. She is here to grieve and heal. Last night, when Briana arrived, she was dead tired, so I let her sleep. It's good you two already met this morning."

"I met Briana while I was working in the vineyard." Kenton opened a bottle of wine. "She was trying to get into the shack...I mean, the cottage next door." Settling into his seat, he smiled at Henrietta. "I also took Briana horseback riding."

Henrietta was happy to see that Kenton was keeping Briana preoccupied. She didn't want Briana to have time to get depressed.

"Miss Henrietta, I slept like a log last night. I woke up early this morning because I was anxious to see where my mother grew up."

Kenton was happy he could help Briana. He knew that she wanted to see her land.

"Miss Henrietta, I made an emotional connection with my mother in the cottage this morning."

Henrietta knew all about Briana's childhood issues stemming from the loss of her parents. Lillie had told Henrietta that Briana was getting into school fights as an eight-year-old. The kids teased her calling her names and making fun of her because she had old people for parents. That Briana had come to terms with the loss of her mother warmed Henrietta's heart.

"I'm glad you made an emotional connection to make you feel whole." Lifting her wine glass, Henrietta said. "Welcome to our home."

Kenton raised his wine glass. Briana raised her water goblet joining the toast.

Ruby entered rolling a tray of skinless chicken breast, seasoned with low-fat Italian dressing, and rice pilaf with undercooked broccoli. Henrietta's doctor had placed her on a low-sodium, low-fat diet due to her high blood pressure, high cholesterol, and Type II Diabetes.

Kenton only tolerated Ruby's cooking because he loved to spend time with Henrietta on Sundays.

Briana critiqued the meal to herself. Her healthy soul food would be a delicious alternative to Ruby's cooking. Briana made a mental note to ask Miss Henrietta if she could prepare some of her recipes.

Henrietta began telling Briana about her grandchildren. Naming them one by one. "I have five grandchildren. Kenton, Justin, Carter, Brandon and Crystal." Before she could tell Briana about each one's accomplishments, the phone rang. Jimmie, the butler, brought the phone to Henrietta. "It's Crystal."

Henrietta stood with her cane and excused herself before leaving to take the call. When she returned, she was smiling. "My granddaughter Crystal just called. I told her I'd call her back later. She's a student at UC Davis studying veterinary medicine. She takes care of our horses in the stables."

Briana smiled when she thought of Beauty. "Miss. Henrietta, your horses are magnificent. I rode Beauty today."

"Beauty is my favorite mare," Henrietta said, proudly. Turning the conversation back to her grandchildren, she continued. "Kenton is the oldest of my five grandchildren. He's in charge of our winery." Henrietta began reminiscing about how she and her husband along with Briana's grandparents listened to Ray Charles records.

Feeling a thickness in her throat, Briana pushed her plate away. Henrietta's stories about her grandparents brought on nostalgic feelings of the good times she had with them. She withdrew into herself by staring at her fork while playing with her cold broccoli.

Kenton saw Briana staring into her plate, and remembered watching her staring into space at the cottage. That forlorn look on her face made his heart sink. In an attempt to change her mood, he offered. "Do you want to get some fresh air and take a walk with me in the vineyard?"

Returning from her thoughts, Briana looked up at Kenton. "That sounds good."

Kenton excused himself from the table. They both walked into the living room and through the French doors.

Briana ran her fingertips along the curling grapevines, as they walked through the vineyard inhaling the fruity bouquet of dark red cabernet grapes.

"Tell me, did you enjoy the tour of your land today?"

Casting aside her sad thoughts, Briana spoke softly. "Yes, I did." Her eyes lit up. "I'm still impressed with that poppy field." Her spirits seemed to lift when she talked to Kenton.

Kenton held his hands behind his back. "Tell me about your life in Louisiana."

Briana's mouth curved into an unconscious smile. "I worked as a chef at 'M' bistro restaurant in New

Orleans. It was on the top floor of Belle of the South hotel." Her eyes had a faraway look in them. "I used to create some of the best meals there." She folded her hands in a pose of tranquility. "Before I got my job, I was a student, at Le Cordon Bleu in New Orleans. My entire day consisted of going to class, coming home, studying, maybe catching a movie on Saturday and going to church on Sunday."

"No way. You lived like that?" He scanned her body. "You didn't have a boyfriend?" Once again, he was surprised at this unpredictable woman.

"I had puppy love boyfriends in high school. But my first real boyfriend was Duane," she said with her eyes cast down.

She continued. "Duane was a Sous-chef at 'M' bistro. I had fun with him sometimes. Everything changed after he left New Orleans to accept a position as an Executive Chef at a resort in Venezuela. After he'd left, I stopped dating."

Kenton gave her a skeptical look. "Duane was a fool." His eyes raked boldly over her. He couldn't imagine any man in his right mind walking away from a beautiful woman like Briana. He asked himself why she stopped dating. Did Duane break her heart? He hoped Duane hadn't ruined his chances of dating Briana. He couldn't compete with an illusion. "So why did you stop dating?"

Swallowing hard, Briana lifted her chin to meet his gaze. "I stopped dating because I was angry at Duane for leaving me. He was my first serious boyfriend, and I didn't ever want to go through that again. She was angry because Duane, like her entire family, had abandoned her.

"You're a good woman Briana," Kenton said. "He had no right to treat you that way."

Briana looked away. "I'm over it now."

"So then you focused on your career?"

"Yeah. I spent most of my time at the restaurant. I spent my extra time cooking at local homeless shelters or senior centers. I had fun trying out new recipes on the residents. I didn't spend much time partying because, as I told you earlier; I'm not a big city girl."

As they walked back into the house, Briana saw that Henrietta had retired for the evening. They walked up the grand staircase and stopped at Briana's room.

"Do you have any plans for next week?" Kenton asked.

"Next week? No, I don't."

"Would you like to get the real flavor of Napa?"

"That sounds interesting."

"I'd like to take you to some Mustard Festival events next week." He looked into her olive green eyes. "I'll be out running errands all day tomorrow, but I'll be here tomorrow evening."

Briana smiled. "What day?"

"The festival will be going on all week. You pick a day."

"Okay. I'll pick one and get back with you. Goodnight," Briana said.

"Good night," Kenton said before walking down the hall. He closed the door to his room. As he lay across his leather sofa, he kicked off his shoes, put up his feet, and thought about Briana. Last thing he remembered before falling into a deep sleep was Briana's olive green eyes.

Later that evening, Briana wiped her eyes with a tissue to hide the tears when she heard Henrietta knock on her door. "Come in."

Henrietta came in and leaned her cane against the pale blue upholstered chair by Briana's bed. Collapsing into the chair as her knees buckled under her heavy weight, she waited for Briana to talk.

Unable to hide her tears, Briana looked up at Henrietta through puffy eyelids. "Miss Henrietta, I am so embarrassed for you to see me like this."

Henrietta sat and listened patiently to Briana. "I know you're grieving for your grandmother, and dealing with the loss of your mother."

Briana's lips and chin began to tremble as she poured out her heart. "My heart aches for Nana, Miss Henrietta. I don't want to be alone in the world."

Troubled by Briana's confession, Henrietta lifted her cataract eyes, while giving Briana a serious look. Pressing her wrinkled hand to her heart, she said. "Briana you're not all alone in the world. You have me, and I'll never leave you."

Briana blinked the remaining tears away. Those were the exact words her grandmother had said before she died. She reached over the side of the bed and pulled out her mother's drawing she'd hidden under the bed. Her eyes brightened a little. "I have some good news Miss Henrietta."

Henrietta was curious to hear the good news.

"Today in the cottage, I walked around my mother's bedroom and found this." Briana held up the drawing. "It was in my mother's closet. My mother always seemed so far away, just out of reach, but I didn't feel like that today. I felt like she was right there with me."

Henrietta's heart softened. She spoke in her softest voice. "Your mother was a sweet girl. I'm glad to hear you made a connection with her today." She took the drawing from Briana and looked it over. "Our loved ones never do leave us, you know."

Briana smiled. "I guess they don't."

"And don't apologize for your tears honey. Remember, I invited you here so that you could heal. You worked yourself into sheer exhaustion taking care of Lillie for so long. I heard it in your voice when I spoke to you on the phone. That's why I invited you out here. I know all about that kind of exhaustion. I went through it with my husband, Frank. I'm only sorry that I couldn't help with Lillie's arrangements."

"Don't feel bad, Miss Henrietta. Nana organized everything so well that there wasn't much for me to do."

"Well, I'm glad you took me up on my invitation. All I want you to do is rest and heal." Henrietta's forehead wrinkled as she thought about Lillie. "I made a vow to your grandmother that I would keep an eye on you if anything ever happened to her." After pushing herself into a standing position, Henrietta leaned on her cane and kissed Briana on the forehead. "Try to get some sleep."

"Okay."

"I'll see you in the morning Briana." Henrietta turned around and walked away.

Briana still felt a little embarrassed, after Henrietta left the room. She walked up to the dresser and looked at her puffy eyes through the mirror. She had cried over her grandmother every night. It was okay that Henrietta knew, but she didn't want anyone else to find out for fear that she would appear weak. Briana walked back to the bed and slipped under the covers. As she lay in bed feeling drowsy, she picked up the drawing again memorizing every inch. She smiled at the bluebird and the crooked letters spelling her mother's name. Hugging the drawing close to her heart she fell into a deep slumber. Her sadness over losing her grandmother, and her happiness over connecting with her mother had just about cancelled each other out. She was beginning to heal.

Chapter 4

Henrietta sat the kitchen island pouring herself a cup of coffee when Kenton walked through the door. "Good morning, baby boy," Henrietta said, greeting him. She only called him baby boy when they were alone. Although Henrietta loved all of her grandchildren, Kenton was her favorite because he was the first born. His parents never had time for him when he was a baby. His father worked all the time, and his mother spent too much time mingling with her socialite friends. That left Henrietta at home babysitting her grandchildren all the time. Henrietta and her grandchildren ate breakfast together many times since they were kids. Henrietta had fond memories of Kenton. At the age of five or six, if he wanted something to eat and couldn't reach it, Henrietta would get it for him and put a big smile on his face. She loved his smile.

"Morning Granny," Kenton kissed his grandmother on the cheek, and poured himself a cup of coffee. Taking a seat next to Henrietta at the kitchen island, he gave her a glimpse of his boyish smile that she adored.

Henrietta was happy for several reasons today. Briana had taken her up on her invitation to come out to visit because Henrietta didn't want Briana to be alone at this time. Also, Henrietta wanted to find out how

Kenton felt about Briana because she noticed how much attention he paid to Briana last night at the dinner table.

Rubbing the small locket she always wore around her neck, Henrietta opened it up. Lillie had engraved "Sisters Forever" on the inside. Memories of Lillie flashed across her mind. They both grew up with no sisters, only brothers. They made a promise to each other, as young mothers, to work at becoming in-laws by becoming matchmakers for their children and grandchildren. They hoped one of their offspring would marry and make them sisters forever. Today Henrietta hoped Kenton would be the one to fulfill her promise to Lillie. With her chin propped up on one hand, she stirred a packet of Splenda in her coffee with the other. "So what do you think about Briana?" Henrietta asked. Her question made him smile.

"She's all right," Kenton replied in a nonchalant voice.

Henrietta raised her chin and gave him a curious look. The smile on his face defied his casual statement. "Okay now, baby boy, be honest, because you didn't act like she was just all right last night at the dinner table."

"What do you mean Granny?"

Pursing her lips, Henrietta gave him a sidelong glance. "Um hum." She spoke in a voice full of skepticism. "You almost broke your neck pulling out Briana's chair last night at the dinner table." Touching the center of Kenton's forehead, with her index finger, she said. "I saw you and I know you."

Kenton had always been straight with her. Why clam up now? "Okay, Granny, I admit it, I'm attracted to Briana."

"Was that so hard to say?" She said.

"You're right Granny. Briana is unlike any woman I've ever known. She's nothing like Tiffany."

Henrietta looked Kenton dead in the eye and said, "I'm going to tell you this one-time baby boy. Don't let your past relationship with this Tiffany control your future happiness with Briana. My advice to you is to get over those shallow women quick, and move on with your life. My gut tells me that you're more than just attracted to Briana."

Kenton knew his grandmother was telling the truth. "I learned a lot about Briana yesterday, Granny."

"How can you know so much about Briana? You've only known her for one day."

"One day can be a lifetime for some people Granny. We spent a lot of time talking in the cottage. I found out that she was an orphan, and her mother grew up in that house that's why it's so important to her. I wanted to hug her yesterday when I found out that she never knew her parents. Did you know her mother?"

"Whoa, cowboy!" she paused for a few seconds to recall her memory. "Briana looks a lot like her mother. Ariana had light hazel eyes and sandy brown hair too." More memories of Ariana popped into Henrietta's mind. "As a teenager, Ariana worked as a Candy Stripe Nurse at Queen of the Valley hospital. She graduated from high school a year early, and then went on to Sonoma State where she met and married that joker Jeffrey Rutledge, who I couldn't stand.

"What was wrong with him?"

"He was an arrogant and controlling son of a gun."

"Tell me about him."

"Well, Jeffrey was from a prominent family from Southern California who owned several mortuaries. Jeffrey's family had a problem with Ariana. They came down to meet Ben and Lillie, and saw how they were living in that small cottage. After that, they threatened to withdraw their financial support from Jeffrey if he married Ariana. All of this happened before the price of land had shot up.

"You're kidding Granny."

"I wish I were."

"Well, at least Briana has family on her father's side in Southern California?"

"Not anymore. Jeffrey was their only child."

Kenton shook his head at their shortsightedness. Jeffrey's parents would have had millionaires for in-laws if they wouldn't have been so snobbish. He was glad Briana never met that side of her family.

Henrietta spoke in a soft voice. "Ariana and Jeffrey died in that car accident two years after they had Briana. Lillie and Ben were heartbroken, over losing their only child, so they took Briana and moved back home to Baton Rouge."

Kenton sipped his coffee as he listened. He couldn't imagine not having any family members left. His heart softened even more for Briana. Looking up into Henrietta's eyes, he said. "I thought I heard noises coming from her room last night. I went to check on her, and heard your voice in there, so I left."

Henrietta smiled at Kenton's concern for Briana. She clapped her hands. "I knew you had feelings for her." A quick thought about her promise to Lillie crossed her mind. It was up to Henrietta to look out for Briana now. "There's only one thing about Briana that I want you to understand baby boy. Hear me and hear me good."

"What's that Granny?"

"I heard you mention at the dinner table last night that you gave her a tour of her land. Just make sure that it's Briana, and not her land or money that attracts you."

Kenton wrinkled his brow. "What makes you think I want her land, Granny?"

"Do I look stupid? I'm eighty-three years old, and you think I'm stupid." Twirling a large ornate gold ring around her middle finger, she looked at Kenton dead in the eye and said. "You've told me a million times that you want to expand the winery. Lillie left all of that land next door to Briana. I don't want you pressuring her to sell her land to you. Do you hear me?"

Kenton cleared his throat. "Yeah, Granny, I hear you. I can't do anything with Briana's land. It doesn't have the right soil and micro-climate to grow white grapes. I'm planning to take a look at some land on the Sonoma coast today where the cool coastal climate will be suitable for growing white grapes. Maybe I'll take a look at some land in the Atlas Peak area later on next week."

Henrietta smiled. "That's good, son." She looked above the rim of her glasses. "Just make sure your heart is in the right place."

Kenton knew his heart was in the right place. He gulped down the rest of his coffee and bounced up on his feet. Before leaving, he said. "Granny, there are two things I love about Briana."

"What's that, baby boy?"

He flashed his handsome smile. "She has the prettiest eyes I've ever seen, and she knows how to cook. I promised to take her to the Mustard Festival later this week."

Henrietta gave him a serious look. "Remember, son, she is here to rest. Don't wear her out."

"I'll remember." Kenton kissed Henrietta on her cheek and left.

Bright sunlight woke Briana up out of a deep sleep. Stretching out her arms, she felt refreshed from a good night's sleep. Her emotional connection with her mother had lessened the grief over the loss of her grandmother.

A wide grin crossed her face. Adrenaline rushed through her body as she thought of her restaurant. Jumping out of bed, she plopped down onto the blue upholstered chair. She began to think about how to get her restaurant started. She could see herself creating original culinary delights again. A group of magazines filled a basket next to the chair. She picked up an Architectural Digest magazine displaying a pale yellow structure on the front cover. "That's how I want my restaurant to look." She thought. She made a mental note to ask Henrietta if she could tear off the cover and place it into a file.

She knew what she wanted her restaurant to look like and had a name for it. Now what she needed was a contractor to tear the cottage down and rebuild her restaurant on the property. She also needed to develop a business plan. Fortunately, she'd prepared many of them as class projects when she attended Le Cordon Bleu. She decided to write down some notes for her business plan but needed some paper and a pen. She opened up the desk drawer in the room and found ink pens and a box of stationary.

After she'd written down an outline for her business plan, she pulled out her cell phone to google a local technology store where she could buy a laptop. There was a store at a local strip mall near the outlet stores. She decided to drive over there later in the afternoon to shop for a laptop. She needed to complete her business plan quickly. Although she had enough money to finance the project on her own, she remembered one of her instructors warning the class that business owners should never use their money to finance a business. In order to obtain low-interest financing, from the bank, she would need a business plan.

After spending the morning writing her business plan, she made up her bed, showered, dressed in a pair of forest green jeans and an olive green cashmere sweater. Taking her car keys out of her handbag, she walked downstairs prepared to drive to the strip mall.

Chapter 5

Kenton climbed into his black Ford F-150 truck, a modern version of Coal and drove to the land auction in Windsor on the Sonoma coast. Kenton's truck towered over expensive low to the ground convertible sports cars crowding the freeway. Kenton rolled down his windows to get some fresh air. He loved feeling the cool coastal breeze blowing on his face when drove down Highway One.

Some wealthy Napa Valley residents hid their wealth by driving old cars and wearing blue jeans and t-shirts. Kenton had adopted this casual attitude. By looking at him, one would never know he was a multi-millionaire. Even with all of his wealth, Kenton still worried that his winery could fail and upset the security of his world. One way to strengthen his winery was by competing with other wineries. In order to strengthen his competitive position, it was critical that he purchase this parcel of land today.

Once he arrived in Windsor he parked his truck on a dirt road and walked to the parcel of land for sale. Kneeling on one knee, he scooped up a handful of dirt feeling its texture. The high-quality soil with its dark color, good moisture and drainage trickled through his fingers. "Perfect," he whispered under his breath. White grapes would grow well in this cool coastal climate. With the richness of this soil, he knew he could expand his winery and produce high quality Sauvignon Blanc, Chardonnay and Riesling wines.

After graduating from UC Davis with an undergraduate degree in chemistry, a master's in viticulture and enology and an MBA, Kenton enjoyed working in his laboratory testing wines and running his family's winery. When it came to Cabernet Sauvignon, no vintner in Napa could surpass his chemical analysis.

He could feel someone watching him. He looked up and saw a man, in the distance, wearing jeans and a white windbreaker, looking his way. It was Peter Keller his rival vintner from Keller Cellars winery. Peter was one man who got under Kenton's skin. Peter was a tall, thin, aging man driven by power. Just looking into Peter's face caused Kenton to remember how badly Peter had mistreated Kenton's father. Arrogant, jealous and accustomed to winning the local wine competitions, Peter humiliated Kenton's father in public many times and played dirty tricks on his father, when Kenton was a boy. Kenton's natural instinct was to ball up his fists and fight his father's battle with Peter. His father told him that the best way to handle people like Peter was to beat them at their own game, by producing a superior product.

Kenton's father, Joe began perfecting his Cabernet Sauvignon until it surpassed Keller Cellars with its superb clarity. Underwood Hill's winery beat Keller's Cellars winery in a local competition. After that, Peter had it in for Joe, and so the cold war began between the two wineries.

The auctioneer started the auction. When Kenton heard the auctioneer's voice through the bullhorn, he joined in on the bidding. He bid on the land for about five minutes. After a while, Kenton saw Peter give him a hostile stare. Kenton widened his legs. After all of the other bidders had dropped out, Kenton and Peter remained. After an hour of raising his bid card to counter Peter's bid, Kenton had reached his limit. He began thinking about how he was going to make payroll and other issues to stay under budget. He thought about the day his father warned him not to pay a dime over the value of land. In those few seconds, Kenton hadn't raised his bid card.

"Going once, twice, sold to bidder 17." The auctioneer cried out.

"Huh?" The auctioneer's voice brought Kenton back from his thoughts. "Bidder 17? I'm bidder 25," Kenton said out loud to himself. Many of the bidders had lost interest and left long ago out of boredom. They would hear through the grapevine, who won the bid.

Kenton walked away from the auction knowing that he'd made a mistake. He was angry at himself for not paying close attention. How could he be so careless? He needed to plant his grapevines. Kenton glanced over at Peter gloating. He subconsciously balled his fists, then relaxed his fingers. He couldn't be angry at Peter for winning the bid. He could only be angry at himself.

On his way home, Kenton rolled down the windows to allow the cool salt air from Tamales Bay to blow on his face. Looking out of the passenger's window, he watched a cloud of fog roll in covering the bay, obscuring his vision. He was also unclear of what the future held.

"I hate bidding." He spoke out in frustration. At the next auction, Kenton promised he would pay close attention until the very end. He wouldn't lose the bid to anyone next week in Atlas Peak, because that was the last parcel of land for sale in Napa suitable for growing white grapes. If he wanted to add white wines to his label within the next four years, he needed to win the auction next week.

Kenton arrived at Henrietta's in the afternoon. Briana was the first person he saw standing at the top of the stairs.

A hopeful smile curved her mouth. "How did your auction go?"

Kenton drew his brows together. He was so sure that he was going to win the land auction in Sonoma. He was too embarrassed to tell her he lost the bid. He glared at Briana.

"I lost the bid."

"I'm sorry. There will be other..."

Before Briana could finish her sentence, Kenton walked out of the foyer. He walked through the French doors in the living room to find solace in his vineyard. Briana stood at the top of the stairs with her mouth open, holding her car keys in her hand. She dropped her keys into her purse. She'd forgotten all about going to a strip mall to buy her laptop. She wondered about Kenton.

Henrietta had been taking an afternoon nap when she heard Kenton's voice. She opened her bedroom door, to find out if he'd won the bid. She saw Briana standing at the top of the staircase holding her purse.

Henrietta's asked. "What happened? I thought I heard Kenton's voice?"

"He lost the bid," Briana said.

Henrietta walked away. "There will be other auctions."

"That was what I was about to say when Kenton walked out on me."

Kenton's attitude could be rude when he became upset. Henrietta had warned him since he was a child about his attitude.

Henrietta shook her head and thought, now he was about to fool around and lose the best woman he'd ever met because of his attitude.

"That's okay Miss Henrietta. He just needs to cool off." Following Henrietta back into her bedroom, Briana had questions about Kenton's personality.

"Come on in and have a seat," Henrietta said. Once inside her lavender bedroom, Henrietta sank into her plush purple recliner. Briana sat on a purple velvet bench at the foot of the bed holding her purse.

Briana massaged her temples. "Miss Henrietta, is Kenton going to be okay?

"Awe honey, he's just mad because he can't get his way."

"Does he always act like that when he doesn't get his way?"

She replied in a raspy voice. "He only gets upset like this when he's frustrated. I wish he would walk away from me when I'm talking to him. I'd knock him out, and he'd find himself picking himself up off of the floor."

Kenton's eyes blazed as he walked off his anger in the vineyard. Slapping a dead leaf still hanging on the vine from last year he thought about his dilemma. Time was running out to plant his new vineyard. Without a doubt, he would not allow anyone to outbid him at the next auction. He would pay close attention and make sure he won.

After walking around, kicking dead leaves and adjusting stakes for about an hour, he'd cooled down. He slapped his forehead when he thought about how he'd walked out on Briana while she was talking. That was rude, and he needed to apologize.

He wiped his hands and then came back into the house. Briana and Henrietta were still in Henrietta's room talking when Kenton came back inside. He walked up the staircase and heard Briana and Henrietta talking in the bedroom. He knocked on the door. Briana opened the door.

With eyes full of regret, he looked at Briana and then Henrietta. "Would you mind if I spoke to Briana alone?" He asked his grandmother.

Henrietta gave him the stink eye, a look of disapproval she gave her grandchildren when they said or did something she disliked.

Briana walked past him to her room. Her olive green eyes had turned dark forest.

Kenton closed the door and sat in the pale blue chair. Leaning forward, he spoke with an apologetic voice. "I want to apologize to you Briana," he paused. "I was rude. I had no right to walk away from you while you were talking."

No one had ever dismissed Briana like that before. Sitting on the edge of her bed, her eyebrows slanted in a frown as she leaned forward. "You're right. You had no right to walk away from me while I was talking to you. I'm sorry you lost the bid, but I had nothing to do with that."

Rubbing a hand over his face, Kenton heaved a sigh, feeling embarrassed for his misdirected anger. "I know...I know. Please forgive me Briana. I don't know what to say other than, I'm sorry."

Briana could see the remorse in his eyes.

"So do you accept my apology?"

"My grandmother taught me to accept an apology from anyone who asked." But Briana wasn't sure if she was ready to accept his apology.

Kenton left Briana's room feeling embarrassed. He knew he deserved every word that came out of her mouth.

Briana closed the door behind him and walked into the bath. She folded a wet face towel and placed it across her forehead after lying down. She decided to buy a laptop at a later date. She fell into a deep sleep and dreamt about a fight she had with Kiara when they were tweens. She could barely remember what they fought about. All she could remember was how bad she felt. Her rude behavior almost destroyed their friendship. Waking up from her nap, she thought about how Kenton had treated her rudely today. Briana couldn't stand hypocrites, so she decided right then to forget the entire incident because neither of them was perfect.

Later that night, they passed each other in the hallway on the way to get a snack from the kitchen. Briana held out her hand to stop him. "I have something to say to you."

Kenton's chin dropped to his chest waiting for her to tell him off.

"I accept your apology. Let's squash what happened today."

Kenton perked up and smiled. "What? You accept my apology?"

"Yes I do. Nobody's perfect." Briana said smiling.

Kenton took Briana's hand and walked with her down the staircase into the kitchen. Briana made sandwiches. While they ate, Kenton told Briana about the Mustard Festival.

Chapter 6

Kenton woke up early Friday morning; the day Briana chose to attend the Mustard Festival. After showering, he chose to wear dark blue jeans and black cowboy boots. He wanted to spend time alone with Briana today. He found her irresistible and wanted to get to know her better. He was becoming more attracted to her as the days passed. He walked down the hall to her room and knocked on the door.

Briana opened her door wearing a white jersey top with white straight leg jeans, accessorized with silver jewelry and silver sandals.

Kenton whistled softly. "Wow. You look fantastic."

Briana brushed aside his compliment. "It's nothing."

"You are the most unpretentious woman I've ever met."

They'd been traveling north on highway twenty-nine for ten minutes when Kenton turned on the CD player. The song Ordinary People by John Legend began to play. Briana closed her eyes, humming to the *song.* Kenton had no idea how much she adored that song and the singer. Singing was a good way to start the day.

They arrived in the upscale city of Yountville, ideal for a romantic getaway. Vendor booths, manned by some of Napa Valley's most prestigious business owners crowded a large field. Briana noticed Kenton waving at most of the vendors as they walked. She watched him wave to his friend standing behind a banner that read, The French Laundry Restaurant. She sampled a few baguette slices topped with gourmet olive oil, vinegar, and mustard. She also took a sampling of some grilling vegetables.

Kenton introduced Chef Julian to Briana. "Briana is a chef. She has plans to open a restaurant specializing in Low Country cuisine."

Briana admired Julian's traditional chef's uniform. She missed wearing her uniform. He wore a white chef's coat, checkered pants, a classic chef hat with a red kerchief tied around his neck. Briana was shocked when she heard Kenton speaking to Chef Julian in fluent French. They both changed to English, when Chef Julian offered Briana a baguette slice topped with Italian seasonings and olive oil.

Chef Julian winked at Briana. "You've got yourself a good guy here." He smiled revealing deep laugh lines around his mouth.

"All right Julian, no flirting," Kenton replied in fluent French returning his friend's smile. Briana turned around and saw that the line behind them was getting longer. Briana nudged him. He turned around and realized they needed to leave. "Everyone wants to come to your booth. I'll see you later my friend."

Julian raised his head, winking at Briana again. "Good luck with your restaurant," he said, handing her a sample of grilled asparagus marinated in gourmet olive oil seasoned with shallots, jalapeno, and cilantro.

Kenton could see as they walked around the festival listening to live jazz that Briana was enjoying herself.

He pointed to a large banner hanging above a row of booths.

"Winery Row." Briana read out loud.

"That's my booth over there," Kenton said pointing to his booth behind a purple and green banner.

He took her by the hand. "Come on." With pride, he led her down winery row. He took an asparagus spear from her saucer, "Um. That's good," he said after taking a bite. "Normally, I work my booth every year. This year, I have some of my employees working the booth."

"Why didn't you work there this year?" Briana asked slightly swinging her arm.

"I wanted to escort you to the Mustard Festival and show you around the Valley."

Briana felt a comfortable warmth cover her face. She appreciated Kenton's thoughtfulness taking time off just for her. "Thank you for bringing me here. I'm enjoying myself."

Kenton gave her hand a little squeeze. "You're welcome."

He could see two of his employees manning his booth in the distance. As he and Briana continued to walk down winery row, Kenton saw Peter Keller standing in the Keller Cellars booth, two booths down from his. Kenton stopped in his tracks. A frown crossed his face.

Briana stopped. She wondered what had grabbed Kenton's attention.

"That's Peter Keller. My rival."

Briana recalled the name. "Isn't he the man who outbid you at the land auction in Sonoma?"

Kenton corrected Briana. "He didn't win the bid. I ceded the bid to him."

"Why would you do that?"

"It's a long story."

Memories of Kenton rudely walking away while she was talking crossed her mind. She hoped he wouldn't say or do something rude today. Glancing sideways, she tried to read Kenton's mood.

"That's my assistant Vanessa manning the booth." He saw her pouring a tasting of his award winning Cabernet Sauvignon for a young male customer. He watched Peter Keller walk over to his booth.

"Come on." Kenton picked up his pace. When they reached his booth, he casually walked inside while Peter was in the act of luring the young man away.

"Peter, how are you doing?" Kenton said in his low voice.

Peter's face blushed upon hearing Kenton's voice. He turned around and gave Kenton a fake smile. "I...I was just asking this young man if he'd like to taste my Chardonnay. But he can taste it later." Peter turned around and disappeared into the crowd.

Briana saw that a line was forming at the booth. She was glad that Kenton didn't say or do anything rude.

Kenton whispered under his breath to Briana. "Caught him red handed." He turned to his employees who were busy serving customers. "You're doing a good job, Vanessa, and Jose."

"You're not going to introduce me to your employees."

"Now's not a good time. I'll introduce you later. Come on, let's go."

As they continued to walk down winery row, Kenton waved to a few vintners manning their booths. "Peter does things like that all the time."

"Things like what?" Briana asked softly.

"He oversteps his boundaries. Peter has an arrogant attitude."

Briana listened attentively.

"I would never walk into his booth and attempt to lure one of his customers away."

They were at the end of winery row. "

Briana squinted her eyes. "Don't you think you're being a bit competitive?"

"My attitude is more of a response to his arrogance than anything else." Kenton lied. He knew he and Peter had a cold war going on. "I may be a bit too competitive, but I can tell you one thing. There's a big difference between me and Peter."

"What's that?" Briana asked.

"When it comes to competition, I'm driven by a strong work ethic." He dropped Briana's hand and crossed his arms. "Peter is driven by pure power and control. He would like nothing better than to buy my winery."

"Why would he want to do that?"

"Because his Cabernet can't beat my Cabernet."

Lowering her head, Briana couldn't believe how childish Kenton sounded.

"He doesn't want me to expand my winery. He knows if I grow white grapes, then I'll beat him producing white wines too."

"So that's why you want to grow white grapes. You want to compete with Peter Keller."

"No. That's not it." Kenton's didn't feel like explaining the reason to Briana today. He came to the Mustard Festival to have fun with Briana, not compete with Peter. He decided to let Peter's aggressive action slide. Kenton liked to pick his battles, and this one was not worth his time. He wasn't going to let Peter ruin his date with Briana.

"Come on, let's go." Kenton walked away from the wine section and didn't look back.

Briana exhaled in relief at the change of Kenton's conversation. But she suspected that Kenton had issues about competing with other vintners that he needed to resolve.

As they walked around the food festival, Kenton told Briana. "I'm going to bid on some land in the Atlas Peak area next week. You interested in coming?" Before Briana could respond, he continued. "I need to plant my new vineyard before it gets too late in the season."

Briana had seen how losing the last auction affected Kenton's attitude, so she had no interest in attending, of all things, an auction with him. "No, thank you Kenton, I have other plans for next week." Right now all she wanted to do was enjoy the rest of the day at the Mustard Festival.

After thirty minutes of sampling more food, Kenton had regained his composure. "Let's walk down this street, toward the music."

Briana felt spellbound by the sound of the music coming from the speakers. As they strolled by upscale boutiques, art galleries, and sidewalk cafés, Briana fell in love with Yountville.

Stopping to rest at one of the empty wrought iron tables in the middle of the elegant city center, Kenton pulled out Briana's chair. "Ever heard of a mud bath?"

Briana slid into her chair. "A mud what?"

"A mud bath." He sat down and leaned back in the chair. "It's volcanic ash." Briana wrinkled her nose. "No. I have not. Mud or ash, what's the difference? They both sound disgusting."

"You've got to try a mud bath at least once. Come on. Let's get out of here. The mud baths in Calistoga are also part of the Mustard Festival." He pulled out her chair, took her by the hand and they walked back to the truck.

On the way to Calistoga, Kenton decided to find out more about Briana's personal life. He wanted to know everything about her and figured this would be a good time to ask. "Can I ask you a few personal questions about yourself?"

Briana had a cautious look in her eyes. "What do you want to know?"

"What do you think about my family owning a winery?"

Briana chose her words carefully, because she knew how important Kenton's winery was to him. "I think your father established a great business for your family."

"I haven't seen you taste any wine today. In fact, I haven't seen you drink any at dinner either."

"I enjoy drinking wine at times. Usually, when I am celebrating something. I learned a lot about pairing wines with food in my culinary classes at Le Cordon Bleu."

"You'll need those skills when you open your restaurant."

"Yeah. I can't wait."

"Tell me about growing up in Baton Rouge."

Briana paused for a moment, wondering why he asked her such a question. Although it was a bit personal, she decided to answer. "I remember playing alone in my grandparent's backyard. I wanted brothers and sisters to play with."

Listening to Briana, Kenton felt grateful to have four siblings.

Briana smiled when she thought about her first day of school. "My happiest day was when I went to kindergarten. I met my best friend Kiara."

"What was so important about Kiara?" He didn't want to miss his turnoff, so he listened while he read the signs.

"Kiara taught me how to fight."

"Taught you how to fight?" Kenton looked over at her. "I can't see you fighting."

Briana relived painful memories. "Kids at school used to tease me." Her eyes had a burning, faraway look in them. "They beat me up and would call me toothpick."

"Toothpick!" Kenton couldn't imagine someone teasing this gorgeous woman calling her toothpick.

Pain echoed in her voice as she admitted. "I never worry over how much I eat because my body keeps my weight in check." Those agonizing incidents had affected her self-esteem for years. She'd never shared them with anyone before. Turning her head away, she gazed through the window speaking in a soft voice.

"Kiara taught me how to stand up to bullies. I poured paste all over this boy's head and made him cry after he kept calling me toothpick." The image was branded in her memory as if it happened yesterday. She glared at Kenton. "That boy never called me toothpick again."

"Good for you," Kenton said. "I like to see women stand up for themselves."

Briana continued to think of how lonesome she felt before meeting Kiara. "I felt so isolated before I went to school. Do you know how it feels to be an only child?" Before Kenton could answer, she said "let me tell you. It's bad when you start to make up imaginary siblings."

"Imaginary siblings, that's not so bad," Kenton said looking for his turnoff.

With a blank look in her eye, Briana said. "It is when you start to name them." Turning around to face Kenton, she gave him a serious look. She studied him in profile as he looked for his turnoff. "You are so lucky to have brothers and sisters, parents and grandparents who are all still alive."

Kenton had never given a second thought about his family because they'd always been there. Compared to Briana, he felt lucky to have living relatives. Her answer to his question threw him a curve. "If these questions are too personal, you don't have to answer them."

"No. They're not too personal. I'm okay."

"Who are the people you admire the most?" He thought she would say the president or Nelson Mandela or some other figurehead.

Briana responded quickly. "My grandparents."

"Why your grandparents?"

Briana remained suspiciously silent. Lowering her head in shame, she recalled a time in her childhood when she didn't appreciate her grandparents. As an impressionable sixth grader, Briana's grandparents embarrassed her on several occasions. She recalled an incident at a sixth grade PTA meeting when all of the young mothers arrived wearing high heels, short dresses, makeup and contemporary hair styles. Her grandmother arrived wearing an old woman's dress, orthopedic shoes, no makeup and her grey hair pulled back into a bun. Briana secretly wished her grandmother was young and pretty like all of the other mothers.

After entering high school, she began to appreciate the sacrifices her grandparents made to raise her. She began to volunteer at senior centers and homeless shelters where she met young people who had no family to support them. After that experience, her only regret was that her grandparents never had a chance to enjoy their golden years relaxing and traveling because they were so busy raising her.

Turning her face away, she said softly. "My grandparents sacrificed their golden years to raise me."

Kenton glanced her way. "I see." He watched her staring out of the window in silence. He figured she was thinking about her grandparents. He thought about how she'd lost her entire family and decided not to ask her any more questions. During their trip to Calistoga, he had learned a lot about Briana's values. She believed in standing up for herself, and she respected her elders. He continued to drive without speaking.

Minutes later, Briana snapped out of her mood. "I have a question for you Kenton."

Kenton's eyes were soft and understanding. "What's that?"

"Who are the people you admire most?"

Turning his head, he gave Briana a gentle look. "You, for one." He paused, looking back at the road. "I admire you Briana," he said, staring straight ahead.

After hearing Kenton's compliment, Briana's mood veered to positive thoughts. Raising a brow, she teased. "Keep your eyes on the road mister." It felt like she'd known Kenton for more than a week.

Kenton paused for a moment. "I admire my father and grandmother."

Briana turned down the music to hear Kenton better.

"My father died of a stroke after I graduated from college. He didn't talk a lot, but when he did, people listened because he, usually, had something important to say."

"You had a close relationship with him?"

"Very close. I'm also close with my grandmother, as you can see." Kenton saw the exit sign for Calistoga. "We're almost there."

Kenton's truck came to a stop in the center of the circle drive to Indian Springs Resort and Spa. Exiting the car, he tossed his keys to the valet before opening Briana's door. They both entered into the resort.

"This is a beautiful resort." Looking around, Briana was impressed by the mission revival style architecture. "It's serene here," she said running her hands through her hair. A huge granite Buddha statue greeted her as she entered into the lobby. Clasping her hands behind her back, she turned around at the sound of a soothing voice.

A young woman spoke softly. "Welcome to Indian Springs?"

Kenton looked at the attendant. "We want a mud bath."

At the sound of the words, mud bath, Briana wrinkled her nose.

Kenton laughed, "I guarantee you'll love it." He pointed to his chin, "See here. If you don't like it, you can hit me right here."

"You've got a deal," Briana said with a skeptical look.

The attendant led them to a room with couples written on the door. Briana stopped abruptly. "Wait a minute. We're not a couple. We want separate rooms."

Kenton laughed holding up the palms of his hands. "What, you don't trust me?"

Briana ignored his laughing. "Seriously. I've only known you for a week. You must be crazy if you think I'm going to share a room with you." Briana came there for a new experience, not for any shenanigans with Kenton.

The attendant led Briana into a separate room. She disrobed and sat in the tub while a therapist layered on warm volcanic ash mud as she reclined. At first, the feeling of being submerged in a thick substance felt revolting to Briana. After a while, the young attendant told her to try to relax. Briana sat covered in the mud trying to unwind. After a few minutes, she opened her mind to a new experience which she was beginning to find remarkably relaxing.

After the mud bath, Briana showered in warm geothermal water, finalizing the treatment with a massage. Changing into short cotton robe, she stretched out on a chaise by the pool. Briana focused on palm trees swaying in the wind and an eight foot granite Buddha watching over her. She listened to soft spa music and sipped on cucumber citrus water.

After his treatment, Kenton walked out of the massage room to join Briana at the Buddha Pond. He sat down on a chaise next to her. His loins ached when he saw how sexy Briana looked with her long legs crossed on the chaise. He wanted to make love to her right there.

Briana gave Kenton a drowsy look while she took a sip of her drink. "That was nice."

"I added extra minutes onto my massage," Kenton said.

Now that they were alone together, Kenton hoped he could sneak in a kiss. He turned his head to take a sip of his drink. He then turned back around only to find Briana asleep in her chaise. After relaxing for a while, he looked at his cell phone. He saw that it had been more than an hour since Briana had fallen asleep. He didn't have the heart to wake her up, so he allowed her to sleep a little longer. After another half hour had passed, he woke Briana up with a deep kiss, which she returned, in her sleep.

Briana's eyes fluttered open to meet Kenton's handsome gaze when she felt the softness of his lips. "I was dreaming." She said.

"Pleasant dreams I hope."

"I dreamt of rolling around in my poppy field, making snow angels. Then you woke me up with your kiss."

Kenton didn't want to talk about her poppy field dream unless he was in it. It appeared as if she was alone in her dream, so he changed the subject. "I hope you enjoyed the kiss as much as I did?"

Briana didn't want to encourage him so she ignored his question. Stretching out her arms, she thanked him. "Thank you for bringing me to this spa. It was a wonderful experience."

Kenton scanned her long legs below her skimpy robe. "Did you find it disgusting?"

"Disgusting?"

Kenton raised his head. "The mud bath."

Looking at him through hooded eyes, she said. "That mud bath was soooo relaxing." Kenton fell under her spell at the sound of her drawl. He lifted his eyebrows. "I guess that means you're not going to hit me."

"No, I'm not going to hit you. I'm going to thank you for a wonderful day."

Standing up, Kenton said. "Come on. Let's go back and get dressed."

After they finished dressing they strolled through local art galleries, and ate lunch at a delicatessen, before driving back home. "Do you have plans for tomorrow?"

"Yes. I plan to spend some time with Miss Henrietta. What about you?"

"I know I already asked you, but I'm going to drive up to Atlas Peak to bid on some land up there. The area is beautiful, ideal for growing white grapes. Are you sure you don't want to come?"

Briana declined. "I don't like breaking promises." Since Kenton had spent so much time with her, Briana wondered if he had a girlfriend. "Kenton, can I ask you a question?"

"Sure."

"Do you have a girlfriend?"

Kenton's eyebrows drew together. He eased his foot off of the gas pedal. "No. I don't have one now, but I did have one several years ago.

"What happened?"

"We broke up."

"Why?"

"Because we had nothing in common. She was a city woman. I'm a country boy."

Briana gave him a surprised look. "I can't see you with a woman like that."

"Yeah, me neither. At first, I was attracted to her. But then, I decided to leave the relationship because our personalities clashed. I also realized we had nothing in common."

Briana thought he must have a high tolerance to date a woman with whom he had nothing in common. A sudden curiosity piqued her interest. Who was his mother? Why hadn't he talked about her before? She made a mental note to ask about his mother at a later time. "So what else happened to cause the breakup?"

Kenton thought Briana was prying a little bit too deeply. He felt uncomfortable talking about the woman who had betrayed him. He couldn't blame Briana for prying, because he'd asked her personal questions on the way up to Calistoga. He decided to keep his answer short. Looking straight ahead, he kept his eyes on the road as he spoke. "Tiffany loved keeping up with the Jones's. I could care less about keeping up with anyone." Turning his head to face Briana, he hoped she heard him clearly. "I'm a simple man Briana. It doesn't take much to make me happy."

Briana decided not to pry any deeper because it was obvious Kenton felt uncomfortable talking about his last relationship. Since he was handsome, and traveled extensively for his work, she wondered if he had women waiting for him in every port around the world. With his good looks, he wouldn't have a problem attracting any woman. After admitting that it didn't take much to please him, she figured he was not a womanizer. Feeling comfortable knowing a bit more about him, she remained quiet. After ten minutes of driving, she fell asleep laying her head on his shoulder for the rest of the ride home.

Kenton thought about Tiffany as he drove home. His biggest mistake was prolonging his hopeless relationship with her. There were so many things he disliked about Tiffany. Mainly she wasn't what he was looking for in a wife. Her flamboyant lifestyle, the mismanagement of her money, and her lack of regard for the feelings of other people. Selfish to the core, he remembered her becoming angry after he'd purchased his ranch. She wanted to live in a high rise condominium, in downtown San Francisco, and spend her time shopping at Union Square. He wanted to live in the Napa Valley near his winery.

Kenton broke up with her after he walked in on her cheating with his best friend, Devon. After that, he became distrustful of women. That was two years ago. He hadn't dated anyone since that happened.

Briana leaned against her bedroom door for support after they reached Henrietta's house. "I feel so relaxed. I could sleep for an eternity" She said through hooded eyes.

"I want you Briana." Kenton looked her over seductively, pushing a thick sandy curl away from her face. Kenton took a step closer and rubbed the back of his hand against the softness of her cheek. He'd known the moment he met her that Briana was the woman for him. He could barely control himself today at the mud bath.

I want you Briana. Those words and the way his voice sounded when he said them carried Briana away into a fantasy world. Leaning against the door her heart almost gave in to his sexy magnetism until a twitch in her stomach snapped her out of her drowsy state. She turned her head away from Kenton. After Duane, she'd promised herself not to get involved with another romantic relationship any time soon.

Kenton touched her chin with the tip of his finger. He turned her face back toward him. He gave Briana his most beguiling smile.

Looking up at him through long lashes, Briana spoke in a soft drawl. "Thank you for showing me around the Mustard Festival today."

Briana's olive green eyes called out Kenton's name. "My pleasure." His voice was deep, almost a whisper.

Briana looked directly into Kenton's eyes and spoke frankly. "I don't want to be in love Kenton."

"Me neither. All I want is a kiss." Amusement flashed in his eyes. But her words felt like a dagger piercing his heart. He turned his head at the sound of Henrietta opening her bedroom door. He reached for the door knob. "Here, let me open the door for you."

After Briana had entered her bedroom, he stepped across the threshold.

Briana held up her hand. "No."

Being a gentleman, Kenton knew when it was time to leave. He gave her one last glance.

Briana smiled. "Sleep well tonight."

Kenton pivoted on his heels and walked downstairs to the library, greeting Henrietta on the way. Once inside, he thought about Briana's statement, that she didn't want to be in love. "Humph! I can change that."

Handsome and charming, Kenton was unaccustomed to female rejection. No woman ever said anything like that to him before. Although Briana's few words pierced his heart, he felt confident that he could change her mind.

Briana closed her eyes, laying in her bed thinking about Kenton's deep velvety voice. Something about his voice made her tingle inside. Although she had no intention of getting involved in another romantic relationship, it was hard to resist this sexy vintner. Suddenly her eyes fluttered open. Why was he so attracted to her? Was it because of her money or her land? She knew he didn't have a problem with her looks, because of all of his complements. She believed she had some attractive attributes. But she felt self-conscious about her figure. She saw her thinness as a flaw. She convinced herself that he didn't want her money because he had so much of his own. He also had no interest in her land, because he was bidding on land all over Napa Valley. So he must be attracted to her personality.

Her thoughts turned to the Mustard Festival. It felt good watching Chef Julian serve samplings of his gourmet condiments and homemade breads. Watching him serve the public reminded her of her old job at 'M' bistro. She couldn't wait to begin cooking again, this time, in her restaurant.

Memories of Kenton waving his hand at the vendors crossed her mind. She knew she needed to be guided by Kenton because of his business expertise. He was where she wanted to be professionally, so she decided to seek his assistance.

Chapter 7

Briana's mind had drifted on and off of Kenton all night. A warm smile found its way through the mask of uncertainty as flashes of Kenton's deep, sexy voice crossed her mind. She shook her head in an attempt to shake off her thoughts. After showering and dressing, she walked down to the kitchen for a late lunch.

Henrietta sat at the dining room table reading the Napa Register newspaper when Briana entered. Looking above her bifocals, Henrietta greeted Briana with a smile. "Good afternoon honey."

"Hey, Miss Henrietta," Briana smiled kissing her on the cheek.

Henrietta squeezed Briana's hand. "Ruby made some sandwiches for lunch. They're in the refrigerator."

"Thank you, I'm hungry." Briana walked into the kitchen and picked up a sandwich and juice from the refrigerator. She returned to the dining room and sat in the chair next to Henrietta.

"Did you enjoy yourself yesterday?"

"I had so much fun Miss Henrietta. That's why I overslept."

Henrietta continued looking at her newspaper. "I'm glad you enjoyed yourself."

Briana's eyes lit up, "Miss Henrietta I want to tell you something."

"What's that?"

"I want to tear down Nana's cottage and build a restaurant. I want to call it Poppy Hill."

Henrietta put her newspaper down, giving Briana her full attention. "Poppy Hill." She smiled. "I like the name. Sounds like a good idea." Henrietta gazed at Briana. "Give me more details about your restaurant."

"Well, Miss Henrietta, I want to open a restaurant with a wrap-around verandah where my customers can sit on the porch in the evening and watch the sunset." Excitement shone on Briana's face, as she gave the details about her dream restaurant, and work as a chef once again.

"That sounds grand Briana." Henrietta was glad to hear that Briana had made the decision to relocate to Napa.

Briana thoughts turned to Kenton and the Mustard Festival. "I have to admit, Miss Henrietta, spending time with Kenton takes my mind off of Nana." Clasping Henrietta's forearm, Briana's eyes softened with an inner glow. "Kenton gave me a tour of Napa Valley yesterday. He takes me horseback riding all the time. I'm beginning to love my land. We always go on long walks through the vineyard. I could go on."

"That's okay." Henrietta patted Briana's hand. She was happy to hear that Briana was healing from her grief. Spending time with Kenton appeared to have lifted Briana's spirit as Henrietta had hoped.

"You know, Kenton is an important man in the Napa Valley business community. He can help you with your restaurant."

Briana agreed. "He introduced me to some of his business associates yesterday. I wonder if he would recommend a construction company to handle the renovations of Nana's cottage."

"He won't mind. Let's ask him tonight at dinner. Here, read this. It's right up your alley." She handed Briana the Fine Dining section of the newspaper.

After lunch, Briana went to Henrietta's library to work on her business plan. After working all day, she walked back upstairs to her room and kicked off her shoes.

Later that evening, Kenton knocked on Briana's door. With the onset of warmer weather, Briana had chosen to wear a taupe sleeveless above the knee sheath, accessorized with pearls and taupe stilettos. She'd flat ironed her hair, and wore it in a simple style which framed her pretty oval face.

When she opened the door, feelings of arousal took over Kenton's body. His eyes slid from her face to her breasts, to her shapely legs. "Wow! You look gorgeous." Every time she opened her door he knew he would feast on her beauty. He thought about it more and then came to the conclusion that it wasn't her clothes that contributed to her attractiveness; she would look gorgeous even if she wore a barrel and suspenders.

"Thank you Kenton." Briana smiled nonchalantly.

Kenton brushed a piece of lint off of his navy sports jacket as they walked toward the grand staircase.

Briana scanned his body. "You look handsome." He always looked handsome to her no matter what he wore.

Henrietta greeted them when they entered into the dining room. Ruby rolled in her tray and served everyone her usual bland meal. This time undercooked carrots, baked skinless chicken and unseasoned brown rice. Briana rolled her eyes at her plate. There was no way Briana could tolerate any more of Ruby's cooking, but she didn't want to hurt Ruby's feelings.

Kenton and Henrietta knew that Ruby was a little slow, so they never complained about her cooking. Henrietta began the conversation. "Briana has decided to turn Lillie's cottage into a restaurant. She's come up with a name for her new restaurant. Tell him Briana."

Although Briana had already told Kenton about her plans, she told him again. "I'm going to name my restaurant Poppy Hill." She winked at Kenton.

To keep Briana's secret from Henrietta, Kenton acted as if he'd just heard the news. He still couldn't understand why she wanted to turn that shack into a restaurant. He thought she should tear it down and build a house.

As an entrepreneur, Kenton had worked many long hours and knew it would take a lot of time and work to open a business from scratch. He doubted that Briana possessed the skills or the stamina to take on such an ambitious project. "Briana, tell me again why you want to turn that cottage into a restaurant?"

"I decided to open a restaurant after I was laid off from 'M' bistro. I promised that I would never work for anyone else again." She stared into space, as she thought about how humiliated she felt when she was laid off from her job. "I'd worked there for five years lifting the prestige of the restaurant, only to be laid off like some new hire on probation." Hurt glistened in her eyes. "After that, I wanted the security of running my restaurant. Now that I've seen my grandmother's cottage, not only do I want to open my restaurant there, but I also want to live there too."

Kenton understood why Briana wanted to live there. She wanted to live where her mother lived. He understood why she wanted to run her own business. She wanted to accomplish something important in life. But, as a wealthy woman, he thought she should consider other alternatives. She didn't need to work to earn a living. She could do anything she wanted. But then, he knew Briana didn't want to live the life of a pampered princess.

"Briana, you know starting a business is hard work. It's going to require a lot of time and energy. Are you ready for that?"

"I've never been afraid of hard work," Briana said, matter-of-factly.

Henrietta agreed with Kenton. "Briana, Lillie and Ben left you financially independent. You don't need to work."

"Yes. I know Miss Henrietta, but sitting around all day doing nothing is not an option. I want to do this."

Kenton knew unless Briana had some help she would wear herself out. He wondered about her business experience. "Wait a minute Briana," he paused. "Have you ever owned a business before?"

"No. I've never owned a business before, but like I said, I've worked as a chef in a restaurant." She said, with a serious look.

Kenton squirmed in his seat. "Yes, I understand you've worked in a restaurant before. But, working in a restaurant and owning a restaurant are two different things."

Briana's desire couldn't hide the fact that she would need hard business skills to run a business. Kenton wondered if she knew the difference between a profit and loss statement and an income statement.

"I do have some business background. I earned a dual degree in business administration and culinary arts from Le Cordon Bleu. My grandmother encouraged me to enroll in the Bachelor of Arts program designed for culinary students opening their establishments."

Kenton and Henrietta listened attentively.

"In the beginning, I didn't think I would need the business coursework because I wanted to be a chef. Now I'm glad I took those business classes, because they will help me when I open my restaurant." She remembered those hard cost accounting classes and those easy human resources classes.

Kenton felt relieved after hearing she had taken some business classes. "What classes did you take?"

"Let's see if I can remember." Holding up her hand, she counted her classes on each finger. "I took cost accounting, financial management, marketing..." She kept going until she counted nine classes.

Kenton straightened in his chair as he listened to her. "Not bad. I'm impressed." He relaxed his shoulders.

Briana gave him a nervous look. "But, I have to admit, I can't remember what I learned in many of those classes. I've never used much of the knowledge for anything. I thought about taking some online business courses to refresh my skills."

"That sounds like a good idea. Your training will all come back, once you begin your classes. It'll be like riding a bike." With the added task of cooking, in addition to her administrative activities, Kenton knew the workload would be brutal unless she hired a manager with strong business skills. He knew about the long grueling hours involved in working as an entrepreneur. It led to his father's early grave. The Napa Valley gave the impression of being romantic and relaxing place to tourists, but as a major player in the international wine industry, Napa Valley could be a bit challenging for rookie entrepreneurs. Kenton let go of his fears because at least Briana had some business training. He believed she was a bright, independent, confident woman, who could figure things out for herself. But just in case she needed his help, he would be there for her support.

Kenton glanced over at Briana. "Is this your first time visiting California Briana?"

Briana looked up from her plate. "Yes this is my first time visiting California as an adult. But, I was born in Napa."

Kenton gave Briana a startled look.

Henrietta wanted to keep the discussion focused on Briana's restaurant. "What kind of cuisine are you going to serve at your restaurant, French, Italian or Mediterranean?"

Briana looked at Henrietta. "Low Country."

Henrietta's face split into a wide grin.

Briana's great grandmother grew up in South Carolina and taught Lillie how to prepare Low Country cuisine. Lillie handed down her recipes to Briana, teaching her how to prepare the cuisine at a young age.

Kenton gave Briana an amused look. He hoped whatever Low Country tasted like, was better than Ruby's cooking.

Briana could read the question on Kenton's face. She reassured him. "It's good."

"Ain't that the truth?" Henrietta said as she ate a piece of her chicken. A native of South Carolina, Henrietta, knew all about that type of cooking with its heavy emphasis on seafood and rice. Henrietta inherited some of her mother's Gullah roots and could speak a little of the language, similar to Jamaican Patois.

Briana smiled at Kenton. "I'm going to serve healthy seafood dishes. I also plan to serve my grandmother's famous southern recipes." Briana saw Henrietta smile out of the corner of her eye. She couldn't read the look on Kenton's face. She knew he was a California native and added. "I might serve some California cuisine too. But, all people have to do is try my Low Country recipes once. Am I right Miss Henrietta?" Briana looked to her for support.

"You better believe it," Henrietta said with hooded eyes.

Briana beamed. "Why don't I test some of my recipes on y'all next Sunday, so you can see what I mean?" She drawled.

"I don't need to see what you mean honey. I know all about Low Country cooking. You're welcome in my kitchen anytime." Henrietta couldn't wait to taste Briana's recipes.

"Thank you, Miss Henrietta, I'd love to cook some of my dishes for you."

Kenton was curious about Briana's cuisine. He loved seafood. Leaning back in his seat, he folded his large square hands across his flat stomach. He'd seen many businesses fail due to inferior builders and contractors. He didn't want Briana to hire a bad contractor, so he asked. "Do you have a contractor to handle your renovations?"

Briana lifted a piece of chicken to her mouth but then lowered it back down to her plate. "No, I don't. Can you recommend one?"

"I have a friend who is a contractor in Napa. I'll give him a call to set up a meeting."

Briana beamed happily. "Thank you Kenton." Her dream was coming together nicely.

Before he could get out another word, Henrietta said, "Kenton can do your business plan."

Kenton gave Henrietta a resentful look for offering his time and expertise without asking.

"Don't worry, Miss. Henrietta. I've started developing my business plan." She had almost completed writing out her draft. All she needed was a laptop computer.

Henrietta gave Kenton the stink eye, daring him to deny Briana his help.

"Briana doesn't need my help. I'll help her if she asks."

After dinner, Kenton pushed out his chair and held his hand out to Briana. "Want to take a stroll through the vineyard with me? We can walk off some of that rubber chicken."

"That sounds good," Briana answered.

He pulled out Briana's chair. "Excuse us, Granny. We're going to take a walk. We'll be back."

Henrietta hadn't taken a nap, so her eyes were half way closed. "I'll be in bed by the time you all get back."

Walking through the French doors, they strolled onto the terrace and then walked down the stone steps. When they reached the vineyard, Briana raised her chin, and walked with stiff strides as she questioned herself. She wondered what would happen if she failed to get her restaurant off the ground. The alternative would be to go back home to Baton Rouge and live in her grandmother's house full of servants, but no family. That was not acceptable to Briana. She wanted to make a new life for herself in Napa Valley where she could open her dream restaurant.

Kenton noticed the solemn look on Briana's face. "I didn't mean to sound so critical when I asked if you've ever owned a business before. I just want you to understand that the Valley is a competitive place."

"You think I'm going to fail in my business."

Kenton reached out to hold Briana's hand. "Have you thought about how hard it will be to prepare your unique cuisine all by yourself? Where will you find people around here who know how to prepare food like that?" He didn't want to talk about who would handle her administrative activities.

Briana pulled her hand away giving him a determined look. "I know what I want to do. When I put my mind to something, I'm not one to give up without a fight."

Kenton believed in Briana's determination, but determination wasn't enough. He knew she couldn't handle the day to day activities involved in running a restaurant and working as a chef all by herself. If she wanted it to succeed, she needed to hire and train chefs, cooks and highly skilled administrative staff. He wondered if she'd ever supervised anyone before. He decided not to ask. He looked up. "Maybe you could teach some local cooks how to prepare your cuisine?"

"That's just what I'm going to do. I have someone in mind who can help me train my cooks." She paused. "I'm going to start with my grandmother's cook and housekeeper Miss Mack. Together we can hire and teach cooks how to prepare Low Country cuisine."

"That sounds like a good idea. Do you think Mrs. Mack will come out here for the job?"

"She helped raise me. She would come to California if I asked her to come."

After their long walk through the vineyard, Kenton walked Briana to her room. "Want some company?"

"I'm still a little hurt over your criticism at dinner."

His gaze dropped from her olive green eyes to her shoulders to her breasts. "I'm sorry Briana. I didn't mean to hurt your feelings. I have a soft spot for you. I just want to protect you. That's all. Let's go into your room and close the door." Kenton asked.

Briana didn't miss his obvious examination of her body. Listening to his velvety sexy voice again made her feel warm in the pit of her stomach. Quickly regaining her senses, she replied. "I'm sorry Kenton, but I don't want to lead you on."

Kenton was unaccustomed to rejection by women. Although Briana was rejecting his advances now, it was just a matter of time before he broke down the iron bars to her heart. Kenton had his pick of women from all over the world who'd easily fallen prey to his beguiling ways. To handle Briana, he needed to turn up the heat to a level she couldn't resist.

Giving her a mischievous look, he kissed her lightly on the cheek. "Want to go horseback riding with me next week in your poppy field?" Kenton thought about his plan to turn up the heat, and then watch her melt like butter in his hands.

Briana smiled as she thought about her poppy field. "Perhaps. But first, I need to buy a laptop. I also need to open a bank account."

"I know the president of the Bank of Napa. I can introduce you to him tomorrow. After that, we can go to buy a laptop."

"Thanks for the offer, but I can handle all of those errands by myself."

Later that night, as Briana showered, her thoughts drifted to Kenton. It was getting harder to resist his sexy advances, but she was determined to focus on her business. She admitted that he was right about her lack of experience running a business. She was glad that he agreed with her idea of enrolling in a few online classes. She decided to take a look at some online college courses during the renovations.

The next morning, Briana, called Mrs. Mack. After offering her the job, she drove to the Bank of Napa. She introduced herself to the lending manager, who helped her transfer some funds from her bank in Baton Rouge to the Bank of Napa. After opening up personal accounts, she began the process of obtaining a commercial loan for her restaurant. She offered to give the manager a copy of her business plan. Briana gave the manager Kenton's name as a reference. The manager knew Kenton personally and was eager to work with Briana as an upcoming member of the business community.

Later that afternoon, she drove to the local strip mall to purchase a laptop computer, printer, paper and other office supplies. Her dream was solidifying nicely.

Chapter 8

Briana looked at three designs with Rex Jensen, a local contractor that Kenton recommended. Briana's eyes sparkled with excitement as she examined the second design, which included keeping the Douglas fir pine tree. She'd imagined her mother hanging ornaments on the tree as a child, during the Christmas season. "Please don't cut down that tree for any reason," she said. It symbolized happiness for Briana.

"Keeping the tree won't be a problem Ms. Rutledge," Rex assured. "I'll need a deposit before I can begin construction."

Briana handed Rex a deposit check.

Rex took the check and promised. "I'll go down to city hall tomorrow, to submit your plans for your building permit."

The next day, Rex drove to city hall to submit Briana's blueprints to the clerk in the building permit department.

The clerk logged in the blueprints. After Rex left, he quickly picked up the phone and dialed a number.

Speaking in a low voice, he said. "Nathaniel, you've got a problem." Glancing around to see if anyone was within hearing distance, he continued. "A new restaurant is opening up right next to the Underwood winery."

"Who's the owner?"

"Briana Rutledge."

"Name sounds familiar."

Seconds later, Nathaniel snapped his fingers. His daughter, Tiffany had told him that her ex-boyfriend, Kenton was dating a new woman in town named Rutledge. He'd promised Tiffany that he would do what he could to help her get Kenton back. Nathaniel also didn't want another restaurant moving that close to his restaurant. Now he had two reasons to run Briana out of town.

"Can you stall the permit?" Nathaniel asked.

"Sure. I can bury the blue prints on the bottom of the pile, just like the last time." This corrupt government employee had broken numerous ethics rules. He'd accepted payments from new businesses owners to have their permits moved up on the pile many times. No payment, no moving up.

"Good. Do it." Nathaniel Young commanded as he took long strides across his office holding his cell phone to his ear.

Nathaniel had bribed people in all levels of government and private industry. His objective was to control any new restaurants from opening up near his restaurant. He'd caused several restaurants to fail by burying their blue prints in the city hall permit department. In Nathaniel's corrupt mind, this carnivorous world ate people alive. He had no intention of being eaten. He would do anything to stay on top.

Friday morning, Rex called to check on the status of Briana's permit. Nathaniel's contact told Rex that Briana's building permit would be held up due to a backlog. Rex called Briana and told her that he would not be able to begin work on her restaurant due to the backlog in the permit department. "My hands are tied Ms. Rutledge. I'll keep hounding them to see if I can get it expedited." Rex began working on another project because he knew the nature of red tape.

Briana's heart sank at the bad news. It appeared as if someone was playing a cruel joke on her. Not one to give up without a fight, she decided to expedite her permit herself. Snatching her cell phone, off of the bed, she called the permit department and spoke with a clerk. She got right to the point. "My building permit has been held up. Can you please tell me why?"

The young woman spoke softly. "We have a backlog in our department."

"Why do you have a backlog?" Briana asked.

"Excuse me for a moment." The clerk put down the phone to prepare for the complaint. She'd taken numerous calls due to the backlog. Her voice was apologetic when she picked up the phone. "Our stack of blueprints gets larger every day. There is a lot of building going on in Napa."

A look of dread crossed Briana's face. "So there's lots of building going on in Napa Valley?"

"Yes ma'am, but I work as fast as I can." The clerk said in a soft voice.

Briana's voice softened. "I'm sure you do. Thank you for your help." Briana wondered if another employee could help get her permit expedited. "Wait. Before you hang up, do you have a manager I can speak with?" Briana's head began to pound.

Nathaniel's contact came on the phone and listened to Briana's question. He remembered when he'd buried her blueprints. "Ma'am, we are trying to handle the heavy workload with our current staffing, but right now we are under a hiring freeze. There is nothing I can do about the backlog."

"A hiring freeze?" Briana muttered. She empathized with the overworked employees, but it didn't help her situation. She was anxious to get her restaurant built. She came to the conclusion that there was nothing she could do about the hiring freeze. Briana was at a complete stalemate. At least she had not given up without a fight.

"I'm sorry ma'am," Nathaniel's friend said.

"Any idea how long I'll have to wait?"

"It could take up to a year even two." Briana paused for a moment before the color drained from her face. She could hear her heart pounding in her ears.

Dazed, Briana hung up the phone feeling a hollowness in her chest. She had a high tolerance for stress, but this setback was causing her head to spin. She thought about storming city hall yelling and demanding to get her permit granted. But it wasn't in her personality to be a cantankerous, loud-mouthed person. She thought about waiting patiently at the doors of city hall in protest, but then she couldn't see herself doing that either. Briana admitted that she lacked the hard business skills needed to run a business in Napa Valley. As a rookie entrepreneur, she wasn't accustomed to dealing with red tape.

Two years, was all she could think about. This single setback had caused a domino effect on her plans. Now, she would have to cancel her business loan. Toss out her business plan. Forget about taking online classes. Withdraw the job offer from Mrs. Mack. Forget about advertising for new employees. Cancel her contract with Rex. Worst of all, she would never be able to live in the same space where her mother lived.

Now that she'd failed to get her blueprints expedited, she lowered her chin and fought her inward battle with defeat. She'd felt defeated before. The shame of losing her job at M 'bistro made her want to hide under a rock. After speaking with the manager in the permit department, she gave up. Her confidence had been broken down to its lowest common denominator. The little pride she had left prevented her from asking Kenton for any more help. He'd helped her enough.

With sagging shoulders, Briana figured since she had no plan B; there was no reason for her to stay in Napa. It was time to pack her bags and go back to Baton Rouge and live in her grandmother's house.

Tears slid down Briana's cheeks as she leaned over the edge of the bed. Her throat ached with defeat. Staring down at her feet, she pressed her hands over her face and cried her heart out.

Forty-five minutes later, she pulled out her Delta Airlines return ticket from her handbag. She picked up her cell phone and saw that it displayed one o'clock p.m. Looking up the next departing flight on her cell phone she found one leaving at seven o'clock. She booked a flight.

Now that she'd decided to leave, she asked herself how she was going to tell Kenton and Henrietta without letting them down. She felt like sneaking out, but couldn't because Henrietta had been so kind to her. She knew Kenton and Henrietta would try to stop her from leaving. But she was too embarrassed to stay. She pulled her luggage from the closet and began to pack her clothes.

An hour later, Briana walked past Henrietta's bedroom. She popped her head inside to say good-bye, knowing that Henrietta would protest. Lowering her head to avoid eye contact, she announced. "Miss Henrietta. I'm leaving."

Henrietta was sitting in her purple chair reading a book. She raised her head at Briana's statement. "What do you mean you're leaving? Where are you going?"

"I'm going back to Baton Rouge."

Startled, Henrietta became instantly alert. "Baton Rouge?" She studied Briana's face. "But, I thought you were going to open your restaurant."

Still avoiding eye contact, Briana replied. "The deal fell through. I can't get my building permit through city hall."

"Honey, there has to be something you can do. Why don't you ask Kenton to help?"

"It's no use Miss Henrietta. I've tried my best. If Rex can't get my permit through city hall, then Kenton won't be able to get it through either. Besides, you and Kenton have already helped me enough. I'm going back home to Baton Rouge."

"Let me get a hug from you Miss Henrietta." Briana left her luggage in the hall and walked over to give Henrietta a hug. "Thank you so much for letting me stay here to grieve. My visit with you made me feel better. I love you Miss Henrietta." Briana turned around and left, leaving Henrietta sitting in her recliner.

She carried her luggage downstairs before Henrietta could get up and stop her.

Henrietta grabbed her cane and strained to lift herself out of her chair. She tried to follow Briana, but couldn't walk fast enough. By the time she reached the stairs, Briana was walking out the door. Standing at the top of the staircase, Henrietta asked. "Aren't you going to tell Kenton good-bye?"

"No. I don't want to face him."

Walking through the door, Briana turned around on the porch, one last time with tears in her eyes. "Good-bye Miss Henrietta." Briana blinked the tears away. "I love you." Closing the front door, Briana took her luggage to her rental car and tossed it into the trunk, and then drove away.

Henrietta walked stiffly over to the cordless telephone in her bedroom. She called Kenton on his cell phone.

Kenton answered. He was busy talking to Tony at Spring Hill Nursery, about his shipment of white grapevines.

"Baby Boy," Henrietta said with great urgency. "Briana's leaving."

Kenton covered his cell phone with his hand. "Excuse me for a minute Tony. I have to take this call." Walking away for some privacy, he asked.

"What do you mean Briana's leaving? Where's she going?"

Weaving while standing, Henrietta walked over to her chair and plopped back down. "She's going back to Baton Rouge."

Sweat broke out on Kenton's forehead. "What happened?" he stammered. "I mean, why is she leaving?"

Henrietta's voice began to crack. "She said she couldn't get her building permit through city hall."

"Uh huh." Kenton paused. "I'll call you back later Granny. I'm going to call her now."

Relieved, Henrietta began rocking in her chair. "Thanks, Baby Boy."

Kenton's expression darkened as panic swept through his body. He couldn't imagine the thought of being separated from Briana. He had to stop her from going back home. He called Briana's number and listened as her cell phone went straight into voice mail. He left her a message to call him as soon as she received his message. Before hanging up, he pleaded with her not to leave before talking to him. After postponing the inspection of his grapevines with the nursery owner, he rushed to the parking lot.

He jumped into his truck and drove straight to the Oakland airport. Since he was a seasoned traveler, he knew the major airline that flew to Louisiana was Delta. He drove straight to the Delta Airlines terminal. He looked at the time on his dash board, and saw that it was three o'clock p.m. He pressed his foot on the accelerator. Once he arrived at the terminal; he looked at the departing flights board, and saw a flight leaving for Baton Rouge at seven o'clock at gate seventeen.

After he had arrived at the gate, he exhaled a long sigh of relief when he saw Briana sitting in a black chair reading a magazine. He hadn't realized how much he'd cared about Briana until now. Without a doubt, she'd found a place in his heart, and he wasn't going to let her leave without talking to her.

Walking up behind Briana, he spoke over her shoulder in his deep velvety voice. "Where are you going?"

Startled, Briana whirled around and found Kenton standing there. "I'm going back to Baton Rouge," she said softly.

Kenton walked around the bank of chairs to face Briana. He towered over her. "You were going to leave without saying goodbye?"

She knew Henrietta was going to call Kenton. She didn't think he would find her so fast. "Henrietta must have told you I was leaving." She turned away from him.

Sitting down next to Briana, he said. "Yeah, she told me. I'm just glad I found you in time." He turned to face Briana. Lowering his head, he pulled her hand away from her lap. He looked into her eyes and spoke in a velvet murmur. "Why are you leaving, green eyes?" He held her gaze. His heart pounded. Briana was the woman he adored. The woman who was trying to walk out of his life. He just couldn't let that happen.

Briana looked up through puffy eyes and answered in a broken whisper. "My building permit is being held up in city hall. I fought like hell, but I couldn't get it expedited. I was too embarrassed to face you after I failed."

"You haven't failed," Kenton said as he took her moist hands into his. He looked up at her through soft eyes. "You should never feel embarrassed to call me." He lifted her hand to his lips and kissed it. "Things like this happen all the time to new business owners. "They play lots of games in city hall." Pulling out his cell phone from the holder on his belt, he asked, "Did they tell you why your permit is being held up?"

"Because of a backlog."

"A backlog?"

Swallowing hard, Briana pulled a tissue from her purse. "Yeah. Rex tried to get it expedited this morning, but he was denied. Then I called city hall and spoke to several employees to get it expedited. They denied me too."

"Did they tell you what's causing the backlog?"

Briana heaved a sigh. "It's due to the heavy building going on in Napa Valley, and there's also a hiring freeze."

Kenton raised a curious brow. His success as a vintner was largely due to his relationships in the business community. He knew the mayor, the city manager and all of the city council members on a first name basis. He pulled up a number in his cell phone. A natural leader, Kenton, had a habit of protecting those he loved. Now that Briana was in trouble, he would protect her too.

"Don't worry Briana. Maybe I can pull some strings." Standing up, Kenton paced in front of Briana as he talked on his cell phone. Someone on the other end answered the phone. "Hey, this is Underwood."

"Kenton, how are you doing?"

Briana's eyes cleared up as she listened to Kenton's conversation.

Kenton explained everything about the backlog to his friend, Tom, the city manager who owed him a favor. Kenton cashed in his favor with Tom. He asked Tom, if he would expedite Briana's building permit for Poppy Hill restaurant. Tom put him on hold for several minutes.

"Kenton, I moved Poppy Hill's blueprints from the bottom of the pile to the top of the pile. It is the next project in line."

"Thanks, buddy I owe you one. By the way, how many projects were ahead of Poppy Hill's?"

"You don't want to know. Let's just say, it's a good thing you called me buddy."

"Okay. Thanks for your help."

"You bet."

Kenton dialed Rex's number. "Rex, I pulled some strings in city hall to get Briana's blueprints expedited. Her permit will be ready by next week."

"Thanks, Kenton, I'm glad you called. I was about to schedule another project. I'll begin working on Poppy Hill next week."

Briana sat in awe as she watched Kenton wheel and deal to get her permit expedited. His negotiation skills were light years away from hers. Turning to Kenton, she asked. "What did you do?"

Kenton laughed with a deep cynical sound. "I got your blueprints moved to the top of the pile."

Leaning back in her chair, Briana gave Kenton a perplexed look. "How did you do that?"

"Let's just say I cashed in a favor."

Briana marveled at how her life had changed with Kenton's two ten minute phone calls. She'd been on her way back to Baton Rouge, but now she could stay in Napa. What would she have done without Kenton? Without his help, her building permit would still be buried in city hall.

Briana stood up and spoke in a soft voice while gazing at Kenton through long lashes. "Thank you Kenton."

Kenton took her small hand into his holding it gently. "It's okay. Come on, let's go back home." Picking up her carry-on bag, he held her hand as they walked back to the ticket counter to retrieve Briana's checked bags.

At midnight, Briana lay in bed thinking about Kenton. Like a modern day knight in shining armor, Kenton had saved her restaurant, with two phone calls. The voice in her mind told her how silly her thoughts sounded. She never thought her knight in shining armor would come to her masquerading as a smooth talking Napa Valley vintner. She chuckled and commanded her mind to quiet down. She would be forever grateful to Sir Kenton Underwood, who proved himself to be a man in her corner—a man she could trust.

Chapter 9

Briana sprang out of bed feeling optimistic now that her restaurant was coming together. Today, as a test, she wanted to try some of her menu items on Kenton to see how his California palate would respond to her Low Country cuisine.

After showering and dressing, she walked down the hall to find out if Henrietta or Kenton had any allergies to the ingredients she would use to prepare her Low Country meal for dinner.

When Briana walked past Kenton's bedroom, she stopped in her tracks. Fresh spring air whooshed through the window sheers. Kenton stood in front of the window with the sun rising at his back. Bare-chested, in all of his glory, he wore only his pajama bottoms as he lifted weights. Her heart jolted when she saw his masculine sexy physique. She gazed at his huge biceps expanding with every curl as he effortlessly lifted each bar bell, like it weighed less than a feather. With each lift, she noticed sweat sliding down the middle of his glistening chest leading to his tight six pack abs. Unable to move or speak, Briana never imagined that Kenton had the build of a Greek god. That this physically powerful man hid all of those muscles underneath his clothing, was unimaginable to Briana. His masculine image burned in her mind, as she fantasized his strong arms lifting her up as easily as he lifted those weights. She imagined him placing her on his bed, kissing her with those succulent lips and making love to her. She stood there gawking until he looked up.

Kenton looked up to find Briana staring at him. "Morning, beautiful." The warmth of his smile echoed in his voice. A flush of heat crept across Briana's cheeks as she rushed away in shame. Kenton lowered his weights onto the floor and stuck his head outside the door. He watched Briana walk down the hall toward Henrietta's bedroom. He called out her name in a loud voice. "Hey, Briana...Briana."

Too embarrassed to answer, Briana kept walking until she reached Henrietta's bedroom. Briana walked through the open door and saw Henrietta sitting in her purple recliner by the window reading.

"Good morning Miss Henrietta."

"Good morning."

"I came to ask if you or Kenton have any food allergies."

"No."

Determined not to walk past Kenton's room, while he was still inside, Briana slowly went over the dinner menu with Henrietta. She'd planned to make a trip to a gourmet store before noon to purchase some of her ingredients. After that, she planned to take a nap before preparing dinner.

On the way to the gourmet store, Briana couldn't stop thinking about Kenton's sexy body no matter how hard she tried. All she could think about was him lifting her up, placing her on his bed, and kissing her with his succulent lips while he made love to her. She felt herself losing sight of her goal of not becoming romantically involved any time soon.

The belief that she had bad luck when it came to love had haunted her soul. If she weakened and fell prey to Kenton's irresistible charms, would he leave her like Duane, or die like everyone else she'd loved?

After returning from the gourmet store, Briana deliberately focused on preparing dinner. There was something about turning on a stove and pulling out pots and pans that made Briana feel happy. Briana was excited to work in a kitchen again.

Briana hummed the words to Electric Lady by Nicki Minaj. She thought about her recipes as she changed into her traditional chef's uniform. She'd purchased a box of plastic gloves at the gourmet store that she would take with her into the kitchen.

After walking downstairs, she passed through the entryway into Henrietta's large pristine gourmet kitchen, to find Ruby sitting at the kitchen island reading, of all things, a Good Housekeeping cookbook. Briana loved Henrietta's Wolf stainless steel appliances, Italian tiles and marble countertops. One would have never known this elegant kitchen existed by tasting Ruby's cooking. Kenton had told Briana that they kept Ruby on, not because of her cooking skills, or lack thereof, but because she was an old friend of Henrietta's. "Good afternoon Ruby." Briana greeted full of energy.

Looking up from the cookbook, Ruby raised her eyebrows when she saw Briana dressed in her professional chef's uniform. "Afternoon." Why was Briana wearing that getup? Was she trying to take her job?

"Want to help me chop some vegetables for dinner tonight?" Briana asked. She'd assumed that Henrietta told Ruby not to cook tonight.

Ruby cocked her head to one side and spoke in her monotone voice, "who said you was cookin' dinner tonight?"

Briana opened the refrigerator door. "Miss Henrietta."

Ruby frowned. "She didn't tell me nothin' bout you cookin' tonight."

Briana listened to Ruby protect her turf. She wanted to win Ruby over, and so she said. "I'm not going to usurp your authority Ruby. I'm just borrowing your kitchen to test out some recipes. I would love for you to help. You're so knowledgeable about this kitchen."

Ruby relaxed. "You can find the pots over there." She pointed to some cabinets near the stove. "The utensils are in those drawers. Let me know if you need anything else."

"Thank you Ruby."

When Briana cooked she paid attention to detail, seldom thinking distracting thoughts. She pulled out garlic, tomatoes, arugula, Spanish onions, bell peppers, mustard greens, and an assortment of other fresh vegetables and began chopping.

Briana pulled more items from the refrigerator and placed them on the counter. When cooking, she moved with the precision of a laser machine, focusing on a task, finishing it, only to move on to the next. She pulled out her smoked turkey from the refrigerator and began boiling it in a large pot. Combing through the pantry, she found the sweet potatoes, red beans, rice, flour, corn meal, sugar and baking powder. She began soaking the red beans in a large pot. Opening the spice cabinet, she pulled out some salt, pepper, smoked paprika, cayenne pepper and placed them on the counter with the other special spices she'd purchased at the gourmet store.

Briana let the water drain from a handful of mustard greens as she lifted them onto a chopping board. After slicing them, she transferred them into a large pot of boiling water with smoked turkey, cayenne pepper, special spices and chopped vegetables. Briana felt confident that her healthy soul food would be good for Henrietta's health.

Briana worked in the kitchen for the rest of the day shelling shrimp, boiling crab and preparing her recipes. She was proud to serve her grandmother's recipes because she knew it brought pleasure to everyone who indulged.

At exactly five o'clock, Henrietta and Kenton sat at the dinner table waiting with eager anticipation for Briana's Low Country meal.

Kenton's stomach growled as he waited. He'd skipped breakfast to have an appetite for this meal.

Henrietta sat at the table with her napkin tucked under her collar sipping water from her goblet while she waited.

Briana gave one last look at her potential menu items displayed on the kitchen island. She transferred them to Ruby's cart. Removing her apron, she walked through the door carrying a tureen of sweet potato crab soup. Later, she rolled out the cart filled with a platter of Shrimp Kedgeree and a large bowl of red beans spooned over steamed white rice. She placed a bowl of Lillie's mustard greens with a platter of cornbread on the table. Then she placed the other dishes on the table. Standing behind Kenton, Briana pointed to each dish, detailing its ingredients. Henrietta knew about all of the ingredients. After saying grace, Henrietta and Kenton began to eat.

Briana announced. "If Ruby allows me, next Sunday, I'd like to prepare Charleston red rice, crab cakes with black eyed pea sauce and seafood gumbo."

Kenton's eyes widened as he looked at each dish on the table. "Wow. Briana, this looks amazing." He inhaled the delightful aroma of each dish and felt like Briana had prepared a feast. He tasted the sweet potato crab soup and thought he'd gone to heaven. "Mmm, this soup tastes good." Seafood was his favorite. He tasted the shrimp kedgeree and complimented Briana again. "The best soul food restaurants in Oakland can't touch this." Briana's cooking went straight to Kenton's heart.

Henrietta said nothing. After moving the bowl of mustard greens closer to her, she dipped a large spoonful into her bowl along with some juice, then picked up a piece of cornbread from the platter. Closing her eyes, she inhaled the hot mouth-watering aroma of the tender vegetable. Pure bliss crossed her face. The mustard greens melted in her mouth just like Lillie's. "I'm in heaven," she said. Looking up with happiness into Briana's smiling face, Henrietta complimented her. "They taste just like your grandmother's."

Briana smiled, loving the way they were enjoying her food. She was glad to give them back a little of the happiness they'd given her.

Kenton grinned broadly at Briana's words; her voice was sweet music to his ears. "If you're going to serve these recipes on your menu, I know your restaurant will be successful."

Pride shone on Briana's face at Kenton's compliment.

Henrietta dipped her cornbread into the greens' broth and raised it high. "Here, here."

At twelve midnight, Briana woke up out of a deep sleep. She'd been dreaming about Kenton again. She couldn't get his magnificent body out of her mind. She couldn't stop fantasizing his strong arms embracing her, lifting her up as easily as he lifted those weights, placing her on his bed, kissing her with his succulent lips while making love to her. Then she snapped out of it realizing it was only a dream.

Turning her thoughts to her restaurant, she decided it was time to get serious and enroll in her online classes. Not one for procrastinating when she had a goal to accomplish, she worked at it full force. Since she couldn't sleep, she removed the covers from her bed and walked in the darkness to Henrietta's antique mahogany desk to turn on the lamp. A chill in the spring air rejuvenated her mind as she turned on her laptop. The screen displayed twelve a.m.

She pulled up a search engine from her browser and looked for online business classes. After opening a website for the University of the Pacific, she filled in the field asking for, areas of interest. "Let's see, business & management," she whispered. A listing of business classes popped up. She saw three classes she wanted to take. After filling in the required fields asking her highest level of education, name, address, email and phone number, she read the disclosure statement at the bottom of the website.

Scrolling down the list to choose three accelerated classes that lasted for six weeks. All required prerequisite classes. Fortunately, she'd taken the prerequisite classes at Le Cordon Bleu. "This is what I want," she whispered. She made a mental note to call Le Cordon Bleu tomorrow and have her transcripts sent to the online college.

Chapter 10

Under a fiery red and gold sunset, Kenton and Briana rode Beauty and Coal, along the trail that led to Briana's poppy field. After they reached the poppy field and dismounted their horses, Kenton removed a Navaho blanket and a guitar from his saddle. He spread the blanket on the damp ground. They both sat down and faced each other. Running her hands across the soft flower petals glistening in the sunset, Briana wondered how anyone could look at a poppy and not feel happy.

Since relocating to Napa, Briana had learned to dress in layers at night. After sundown, she knew the weather would turn cool. She chose to wear a pair of blue jeans, an olive V-neck cashmere sweater, and an olive wool scarf wrapped around her neck underneath a wool jacket.

Kenton slid the scarf from around her neck and placed it on the blanket. Picking a single poppy, he slid it over her right ear and thought he'd never seen a more beautiful woman. Leaning forward, he caressed her cheek with the back of his hand and spoke in his deep voice. "I have something to confess to you Briana."

The sound of his sexy voice along with the scent of the fresh spring air made her head spin. Looking at him through hooded eyes, she asked. "What do you have to confess?"

Although Kenton had recurring dreams of them making love, he remembered Briana saying that she didn't want to be in love. He would never admit it, but those words had pierced his heart. All he wanted to do right now was take Briana into his embrace and make love to her. "I've been attracted to you since the moment I met you."

Briana laughed when she thought about the day they met. She corrected him. "The moment you met me, you called the police."

"No, I didn't." Kenton denied.

"You dialed 911."

"I was just playing. I wanted to get to know more about you when I saw you sitting on that broken door."

"I would've never known." Feeling her heartbeat racing, Briana returned the accolade. "I thought you were handsome."

He took her hand into his, speaking with light sarcasm. "You broke my heart when you told me you didn't want to be in love."

Briana had forgotten she'd said that. "I promised myself not to get involved with another relationship after Duane left."

Kenton was right. Duane had broken her heart. "I guess I have to pay for Duane's mistake."

"No Kenton. You're wrong." She paused. "It's not that I don't want to be in love. It's simply that I want to focus on reviving my career right now."

Kenton's eyes glowed. "Thanks for clearing that up." Now that Kenton knew Briana hadn't ruled out love altogether, he felt optimistic. He remembered his plan to turn up the heat. The best way to do that was by singing her a love song. He picked up his acoustical guitar, while looking softly into her eyes. "I have a song I want to sing to you."

There was something warm and alluring in his voice. Looking at him through soft eyes, Briana wondered if he could sing.

Kenton expertly thumbed the strings on his acoustical guitar and began singing the song, Besame Mucho in Spanish.

Briana felt mesmerized by the song. She became instantly aroused listening to his silky voice sing while he interpreted the words into English. He continued playing his guitar. "This song is about being kissed passionately."

Briana had an intense look in her eyes as she listened to his song. Lulled by his sexy voice, she observed how masterfully his fingers moved across the strings with no effort. He sang the second and third verses. After ending the song, he put down his guitar, pulled Briana into his embrace, and began kissing her passionately.

No longer able to resist the advances of this sexy vintner, Briana returned his kiss feeling a burning desire below her stomach, with an aching need for more. She felt shocked at her eager response to the touch of his lips. Her mind told her to stop, but the warmth of his kiss told her to continue. He forced her lips open with his thrusting tongue. She responded to his intoxicating kiss with slow silky kisses. She felt the heat in her body rise. Gathering her tighter into his powerful embrace, Kenton laid her back onto the blanket moving his large square hands up and down her torso, around her waist, down her hips to her thighs. Her heart jolted as he moved his warm, calloused hands under her sweater. Briana enjoyed the warmth of his embrace around her body. Sliding her arms inside his jacket, under his shirt, she caressed Kenton's magnificent muscles. Laying this close to his body, Briana thought she would faint from the rapture of his intoxicating kisses. His lips moved to her soft neck, searing hot kisses down to her throat. She tried to throttle the dizzying current racing through her body, but his smoldering kisses set her aflame. After the long kiss, their bodies settled in exquisite harmony under the universe as they gazed at the silver stars in the black sky. Now that the sun was gone, the weather had turned cool. Kenton felt Briana shiver in his arms.

"Getting cold?" Kenton's left eyebrow raised a fraction. "I know how to keep you warm."

Briana expected him to pull her closer to him. Instead, he stood up and pulled another Navajo blanket from his saddle, unrolled it and placed it over her shoulders.

"Thank you. This field is a special place for me." Briana said.

"I know you love this place," Kenton said.

"No, it's more than just special. This field has an otherworldly feel to it. I want to build a white gazebo in this exact spot and dedicate it to my family. No need to surround it with fancy rose bushes, because, in my opinion, no flowers in the world can compare to these little orange poppies."

Kenton's mouth curved into a smile. "I think you'd honor your family well by building a gazebo in this field." Picking up the rumpled damp blanket which had become entwined with Briana's scarf and his guitar, he whispered. "Let's go."

That night Briana lay in bed thinking of Kenton's steamy hot kisses and his romantic love song. She'd broken the promise she'd made to herself after Duane left. She could no longer resist this sexy vintner who set her body, mind and soul on fire.

Chapter 11

Kenton could hear his foreman, Tim, barking out orders to the workers, first in English and then in Spanish. Standing on top of Atlas Peak, Kenton looked into his vineyard and saw Tim bending up and down, as he hammered stakes into the earth. To control worker's compensation problems, Kenton had told Tim many times that he had to be an example for the workers. He discouraged him to work shirtless or hatless in the sun. The only two workers who heeded Kenton's warning was Vanessa's two brother's Jaime and Jose who protected themselves by wearing white t-shirts and straw cowboy hats when they worked in the vineyard.

"I'll see you tomorrow morning." Jaime said to Kenton as he and Jose drove off.

Kenton splashed some water on his face from a bucket. He looked up. "Okay guys. See you tomorrow."

"The weather might suddenly change overnight." Tim warned as he walked away with his t-shirt slung over his back.

"See you tomorrow morning Tim." Kenton didn't care if the weather changed. His vines needed watering anyway. Nothing could spoil his day, because he'd achieved his goal of planting his vines on time. He jumped into his truck and drove off.

A weary Kenton drove his truck back to his ranch. Halfway there, the first droplet of hail bounced off of his windshield. The closer he came to his ranch, the harder the hail hit. By the time he pulled up to his front door, the entire driveway was covered with hail. Dead tired from planting vines all day, Kenton rarely felt anger toward mother-nature, but now he cursed under his breath. "Humph." He huffed. "Just my luck, this hail storm would happen now."

Kenton felt disappointed. He'd worked months on his winery expansion only to have it destroyed by balls of hail in one day. He didn't think the vines would survive overnight.

Drawing a hot bath, he sank into the tub and fell asleep. He was awakened by his cell phone lying on a chair next to the tub. He picked up the phone and heard Briana's voice.

"Kenton, I called because of the hail storm. Is it going to affect your vineyard?

"Don't worry about it. The vineyard will be okay."

"I'm sorry Kenton. How are you? You sound tired."

"I'm fine."

"This is just a temporary setback isn't it?" Briana could hear a slight disappointment in his voice.

"Yeah. If the vines survive, I can have the workers adjust them tomorrow. Just depends on how long the storm lasts and the damage the hail will cause."

"I'll go with you tomorrow, to check on the damage." Briana offered.

Kenton wiped his face with a steaming hot towel. "That's not necessary."

"But, I want to go with you. In fact, do you want some company now? I can come over and give you a massage."

"A massage sounds good. Come on over, baby. I'll leave the front door unlocked."

Thirty minutes later Briana walked through the front door. Kenton met her in the living room wearing a towel wrapped around his waist. The hot bath had melted away most of the tension he'd felt.

Briana took one look at Kenton and saw the sleepiness in his hooded eyes. "Come on let's go into your bedroom." She took him by the hand.

Kenton lay across his large bed on his stomach with his head hanging over the side. "Talk about setbacks." Kenton moaned.

Kneeling in front of him, Briana began massaging his shoulders. "I know firsthand about disappointment and setbacks. Remember?" Briana smiled, kissing his forehead. "I felt disappointed when they delayed my permit. But then, you, Sir Kenton, came in and saved the day. I don't know what I would have done without you. Now I'm here to save you with my massage."

Kenton was falling asleep. He couldn't think of Briana's words only her touch. "Emm. That feels so good. I love your touch, Briana."

Briana stood up, and began massaging him along the edge of his spine.

Kenton wanted to grab her and make love to her right there, but he was beat.

When she reached his lower back, and pressed down, he said. "Ooh baby, that feels good." Moments later, he said. "Don't worry about the vineyard. Vintners have to deal with weather related issues all the time." Briana's voice had lulled him into a deep sleep.

Briana continued to massage his shoulders. Kneeling in front of him again, she looked at his closed eyes and heard a snore. Laughing, she turned him around on the bed. She covered him with a fur throw from his corner chair, and left as quietly as she came.

The next morning Briana rode with Kenton up to Atlas Peak to check on the vineyard. She saw that his employees expertly re-attached some of the surviving vines to the stakes.

Kenton walked around the vineyard inspecting each row of vines. Walking back to the truck, he said to Briana. "The vineyard looks good. Not a lot of damage."

Briana relaxed when she heard the good news. Stepping out of the truck, she gave Kenton a wide grin. "Thank goodness your vineyard is okay." Now that his vineyard was no longer in danger, Briana could relax.

After an hour had passed, Briana turned her attention to her restaurant. "Are you going to work up here for the rest of the day?"

"No. The workers have everything under control. Why do you ask?"

"I want to stop by the cottage to take a look and see how the demolition is coming along. It should be finished today."

"Do you want me to come with you?" Kenton asked.

"I'd love for you to come."

They drove from Atlas Peak to the cottage. Excitement ran through Briana's veins like cold ice water. She couldn't sit still in the truck. More than anything in the world, she wanted to see construction begin on her dream restaurant. When they pulled in front of the construction site, Briana saw that the cottage had been demolished. All that remained standing was the majestic Douglas fir pine tree that she loved so much.

Kenton instinctively wrapped his strong arm around Briana's shoulders as they stood before what remained of the cottage. He remembered how emotional she felt standing in her mother's bedroom. He looked into her eyes, and asked. "You okay?"

"Yeah, I'm fine."

Kenton tightened his embrace around her shoulders and kissed her cheek as they watched the crew cleanup the last of the debris. He walked across the yellow tape, and picked up a small piece of hot pink plaster and brought it back to Briana. "Here. Keep this as a souvenir to remember your mother's bedroom."

Happiness glowed in Briana's eyes. "Thank you," She said, slipping the souvenir into her purse. They turned around and walked back to the truck.

Chapter 12

The five thousand acre Underwood Hills winery housed production facilities, offices, gift store, delicatessen, and a hospitality center. Visitors could taste Underwood Hills' signature Cabernet Sauvignon, and take a tour or have a private tasting with Vanessa Jimenez, the senior wine educator. Although the outside patio offered visitors incredible views of the valley, the interior of the winery was also elegant and comfortable. On cold, foggy days when the weather was unsuitable for sitting outdoors, Kenton offered tastings indoors, complete with a cozy fireplace. He offered tastings by the glass or bottle every day beginning at eleven thirty in the morning.

Kenton saw Vanessa washing glasses and setting up the bar in the tasting room on the way to his laboratory.

Vanessa waved her hand. "Morning, Mr. Underwood."

Kenton had asked Vanessa to call him by his first name many times. Vanessa thought it was disrespectful to address her employer by his or her first name. Kenton waved. "Morning Vanessa."

Kenton walked with quick steps downstairs to the cellar. After reaching his laboratory, Kenton slipped on his white lab coat. He grabbed two decanters from the shelf above the sink. He walked over to the wine reserves stored in huge oak aging barrels stacked on top of each other. Each barrel had a valve attached to its side to release the wine for testing. Kenton drizzled samples into both decanters and took them back to his laboratory. He began analyzing and testing the wine's various chemical compounds.

As a chemist and winemaker, Kenton knew that each year's reserve was different, depending on drought, flooding, or early frost. He'd already tested one of his best year's reserves and entered it into the International Wine and Spirit Competition coming up in Italy. He knew the judges would be analyzing his submission based on clarity. One way he ensured his wines would pass all types of blind tasting tests was by making sure they were clear.

It was after one o'clock. Kenton came up from his laboratory to the hospitality center to have lunch with Briana in the delicatessen. When he reached the top of the stairs, he saw Briana's car pull into the parking lot. He rushed through the tasting room to open the car door for Briana. "Good afternoon beautiful. Hungry?"

"Yes and I'm starving. I skipped breakfast."

Kenton smiled, "Come on, let's get some lunch."

Vanessa was bending down putting away glasses when they walked through the door.

After ordering sandwiches and salads in the delicatessen, Kenton and Briana found seating at a wrought iron table in the middle of the dining area.

Kenton pulled out a chair for Briana. "Come over here Vanessa. I have someone I want you to meet."

Vanessa picked up a dish towel to dry her hands. She left the tasting bar and switched on the ceiling fan. The tasting room had turned warm

"Dios Mio." She complained about the heat in Spanish before walking over to their table.

Kenton introduced them. "Briana, this is Vanessa Jimenez, my assistant. Vanessa, this is Briana Rutledge. She's going to open a restaurant next door."

"Nice to meet you." Briana held out her hand, her smile reaching her eyes. She could see the look of approval on Vanessa's face as their eyes met. Although Vanessa possessed ordinary facial features, she carried herself with poise and dressed well.

"The pleasure is mine," Vanessa broke into an open, friendly smile after hearing the news while shaking Briana's hand.

"I'm training Vanessa to take over the tasting bar and the cellars." Some new customers walked into the tasting bar.

Vanessa kept an eye on the new customers. "Mr. Underwood treats us all like one big family around here. He is a pillar of the community." She squinted her eyes and smiled at Briana. "Good luck with your restaurant. I better look after our customers." Vanessa walked back to the tasting bar.

Kenton took a bite of his sandwich. "Vanessa and her brothers have been working here since I was in high school. She just graduated from UC Davis with a degree in Viticulture and Enology."

"Wow. She's smart." Briana said piercing a cherry tomato with her fork.

"Yeah, she and her brothers are from El Salvador. They are like family. Her brothers work with me in the vineyard." He turned his attention to Briana's outfit. "I meant to tell you that you look fabulous today."

"Thanks," Briana said. She was wearing a white linen sheath with nude stilettos.

"You made me a promise."

"What?"

"You promised to cook a Low Country meal for me at Sage Creek?"

Briana paused for a moment. "Oh yeah, I did make that promise. I can cook for you tomorrow night." Briana glanced at Vanessa pouring wine for customers. She paused, turning her head again, when she noticed Vanessa standing in front of a wall covered with awards from top to bottom and side to side leaving no space between each award. Her inner voice cut through her thoughts. Kenton must have worked hard to win all of those awards. "He must be very ambitious to be that successful," she whispered under her breath.

"What." Kenton didn't catch what she'd said.

"Nothing," Briana said. She paused for a moment. "I was just admiring all of your awards. I was saying you must be very ambitious to win all of those awards."

"Yes. I am very ambitious."

"I guess winning is important to you."

"Yes it is."

"Oh. I see." Briana twirled the last piece of lettuce on her plate. She'd caught a glimpse of his competitive behavior at the festival when Kenton ran Peter Keller out of his booth. She was glad the wall was there because it revealed a lot about Kenton's personality. It showed that winning was important to him. It reflected how serious he was about running his successful winery. For those reasons, she was glad. But she wondered if his competitive habits would spill over into their relationship. Would winning become more important than the time they spent together? She thought that would be a difficult thing to face.

"My father won most of those awards." Kenton took a bite of his crispy pickle. "In order be a top wine producer in the Valley, I must compete in a lot of wine competitions.

"Oh. I see." She paused. "It just that…"

"What? Tell me."

"Well to me, the wall reveals a lot about you as a person."

Crossing his arms over his chest, Kenton turned around in his chair to examine the wall. No one had ever said that to him before. "So what do you think it reveals?"

"That you are competitive, ambitious. That you like to win."

"What's wrong with winning?" Kenton thought Briana was becoming a bit too nosey, prying into something she didn't understand. Yes, he was competitive and ambitious. And yes, he liked to win. What was wrong with that? He wasn't accustomed to explaining anything about his winery to anyone. Who did she think she was?

"Nothing is wrong with winning. It is a good thing." She paused thinking she was prying. Maybe she should wait until he opened up to her. "I'm sorry; I shouldn't have said anything. Your wall is great."

Leaning away from Briana, Kenton looked at the wall again. "So you think it reveals a lot about my personality."

"Only good things," Briana said.

Kenton could tell from Briana's body language that she disapproved of the wall, no matter what she said. He felt insulted by her critique, and didn't want to talk about it anymore. "Look Briana. I have to go. I have some work to do in the vineyard today. Maybe we can talk about this later."

"Sure." Briana could hear a slight annoyance in Kenton's voice. She rose in one fluid motion from her seat. "I'll see you later." She walked out of the delicatessen.

Kenton stood at the table, and watched Briana walk out the door. After watching her drive away, he walked behind the bar. "Vanessa, why don't you take a break? I'll take over pouring wine." Turning around to face the wall he asked Vanessa. "Before you leave. Tell me. What do you think about this wall?" he said pointing to his awards.

"I don't know." Vanessa thought the wall looked tacky, but she couldn't say that to Kenton. She didn't feel it was appropriate to criticize her employer, even if he asked. To avoid answering his question, she lowered her eyes, hunched her shoulders, and walked away.

Kenton was embarrassed when he realized that Vanessa avoided answering his question. Maybe he shouldn't have put her on the spot like that. Taking a good look at his twelve foot wall, full of awards, he thought, maybe there was something to Briana's observation. Maybe it was time to take a few down.

Hours later, he admitted that Briana was right, and Vanessa was too afraid to say what she thought. Kenton needed to apologize once again to Briana.

Chapter 13

Kenton knocked on Briana's door later that evening. Briana leaned back on her elbows in the bed when she heard the knocking. "Come in."

Kenton walked in feeling embarrassed more than anything. "May I sit down?"

Briana pointed to the powder blue chair. "Sure. Have a seat."

Kenton had rubbed the back of his neck before he sank into an overstuffed chair. "Briana, you made a good observation about that wall today. I'd never thought much about it, but that wall does reveal a lot about me. Your conversation hit home. I want you to understand the deeper reason all of those awards are up there."

Briana sat up in the bed to listen closely. She'd thought he was in total denial.

Leaning forward in the chair, Kenton grasped his hands together. "That wall is a reflection of my father's obsession that I have internalized over the years. I never put much thought to it until now, because no one has ever brought it to my attention."

Honesty was important to Briana. She looked at Kenton with new understanding. Moving to the edge of the bed, she leaned forward. "Thank you for being honest Kenton. I knew there was something you didn't want to talk about then."

Kenton wanted to be open and honest with Briana. He poured his heart out beginning with his father. "When my father started our winery, Peter Keller was the only vintner in the valley who criticized my father's winemaking abilities at local wine competitions." He rested the palms of his hands on his knees. "Peter had no problem criticizing or humiliating my father in front of me, as if I were invisible. As a twelve-year-old, I witnessed Peter humiliate my father so many times, that I stopped counting. My father just brushed it off, but being a daddy's boy, I balled up my fists and wanted to fight Peter. My father told me the best way to fight people like Peter was by beating them at their own game."

Standing up, Kenton walked over to look out of the window. He looked at the stars as if he were looking back in time. He continued telling Briana how his father worked hard, day and night, learning how to make the best Cabernet wine in the valley. "When my father finally beat Peter's Cabernet in a local competition, Peter quit criticizing him in public because all of the other vintners acknowledged my father's superior winemaking skills. Now whenever I run into Peter Keller, I feel like that twelve year old boy with his fists balled up ready to fight. When it comes to Peter, I get real competitive."

"But since I met you Briana, you've challenged me to see myself from a different perspective." Standing up, he put his index finger under her chin, reading her upturned face, he said. "I promise you Briana, I'm going to deal with my competitive attitude."

Briana felt like she'd met the real Kenton. Looking up at him through long lashes, she said. "It sounds like you've been fighting your father's battle."

Kenton hunched his shoulders. "Seems like it."

"Maybe your father fought that war with Peter Keller to make life easier for you."

"Yeah, maybe so." Kenton didn't tell Briana that he had a bone to pick with Peter. He remembered how Peter had recently antagonized him by luring away his customer at the festival. Kenton made a mental note to confront Peter Keller once and for all. It was important to stand up to bullies. Some people only knew violence and aggression. Kenton's thoughts turned back to Briana. "I thought you might understand my dilemma if you understood my father and our close relationship."

Feeling relieved, Kenton exhaled a long sigh. After opening up to Briana, he felt like a new man. Peace and contentment filled his spirit. Looking into Briana's eyes, he knew, he was the luckiest man in the world to have her.

Now that Briana understood why Kenton was so competitive, her heart rang out with joy. She beckoned him with her eyes.

By instinct, Kenton replied to her unspoken request. Sitting next to her on the bed, he pulled her into his embrace, brushing a gentle kiss across her lips. Then his mouth covered hers with a deep kiss.

"I'm sorry for prying," Briana said between kisses.

"I've never shared that story with anyone, not even my grandmother." Unspoken happiness was alive and glowing in his eyes.

Briana buried her face against his massive chest. "Honesty is important to me."

Kenton leaned back, staring her in the eye. "Honesty is important to me too."

Briana swung into the circle of his embrace sitting on his lap.

"I guess you're not angry with me anymore?" He asked.

Wrapping her arms around his neck, Briana replied. "No, I understand you better now."

Kenton kissed the side of her face and down her neck as his hand found the zipper to her white linen dress. He slid the zipper down, pulling the dress from her shoulders. His fiery hot fingers unfastened the back of her lacy bra, searing a hot path down to her tiny waist. Pleasure radiated outward from Briana as she felt the heat from his hands. Reclaiming her lips, he pushed her down onto the bed. Her voice shattered with the hunger of his kisses.

"Kenton!" She cried out.

"What baby." He said enraptured with her kisses.

"We can't do this here."

A frustrated Kenton sat up on the edge of the bed. He couldn't do this anymore. His body ached for Briana, and he couldn't wait any longer. "Let's go to my ranch." His gaze dropped from her eyes to her shoulders to her breasts. Picking up her lace bra he'd unfastened, he handed it to her and said. "Let's go now."

"Okay."

Kenton stood on his feet and picked up her white linen dress. He handed it to her with one finger. Leaning against the closed door, he watched her get dressed.

"Wait a minute. What are we going to tell Miss Henrietta? Won't she miss us?"

Kenton laughed. "My grandmother is a grown woman. She knows all about love, and she knows how I feel about you. Believe me, she'll understand if she doesn't see us for dinner."

Pitch black darkness filled the sky by the time they reached Sage Creek. An undeniable magnetism had been building between them. Kenton couldn't keep his mind off of his green eyed beauty. Opening the passenger door, he took Briana's hand to help her down.

Briana gave him a seductive look.

His gaze was as soft as a caress.

As they walked to the front porch, Briana seemed to drift along on a cloud. She could feel the firmness of Kenton's body as he stood behind her inserting his key into the front door. She turned around under the bright porch light and gave him a slow languid kiss.

Kenton stood there for a moment rubbing his cheek against the softness of Briana's neck imagining her lying across his bed. He pushed the door open and turned on the lights.

Briana walked into the large living room, recalling the rustic beauty of his ranch, which made her feel completely at ease.

Kenton plopped down on his leather sofa, patting the seat next to him. "Have a seat."

Briana sat down next to Kenton.

"Want some wine?"

"Sure, I'll have a glass."

Kenton walked over to the butler's pantry to select a bottle of wine. He grabbed two red wine glasses, a corkscrew and walked back to the sofa. He walked over to his Bose docking station and selected the John Legend song;Best You Ever Had from his iPod. As the music began to play, and the base thumped, Kenton sang along with the song.

The excitement of hearing Kenton's rich baritone voice singing along with the music added shine to Briana's eyes. She watched Kenton hold out his hands beckoning her to dance with him.

Kenton pulled Briana up from the sofa. "Come on, baby, let's dance." A faint light flickered in the depths of his eyes when he pulled her up, holding her around her waist. He pressed her body close to his, dancing, spinning, swaying and dipping her.

Briana realized he was stepping Chicago style. Determined to keep up with his pace, Briana felt dizzy following his lead. She hadn't stepped in a long time, but the movements came back, like riding a bike. Briana felt alive dancing in Kenton's arms.

Kenton complimented her. "You're a good dancer," he said, holding her in his embrace. He continued to sing along with the song.

Briana grinned and leaned her head back in delight.

He slowed down, pulled her close and sang into her hair.

"You remembered my favorite artist." Briana closed her eyes as she laughed. The sound of the music, the smoothness of Kenton's dancing and singing fascinated Briana. Kenton was the best man she'd ever known.

"How could I forget?" Kenton said in between singing words to the song.

Briana began to sing along with Kenton. They sang her favorite part simultaneously with loud voices. Briana paused for a few seconds which felt like an eternity. Within seconds, she snapped back into real time. She felt as if she'd been hanging in space for hours. Looking into Kenton's eyes, she melted in the tenderness of his gaze.

Kenton twirled her around and then pulled her close again. Staring into her eyes, he gave Briana a smoldering look. "How did you like that?" They stopped dancing, but he still held her close.

Kenton's deep, sexy voice sent a ripple of awareness through Briana's body. He casually slid his hand down her back, while pressing his lips against hers.

Briana returned his hot kisses as a tingling ecstasy settled in the pit of her stomach, burning through her inside out.

Kenton looked Briana over seductively, whispering into her hair, "I've wanted to make love to you since the first day I saw you Briana." He whispered.

Briana's emotions whirled and skidded into oblivion as she listened to Kenton's sexy voice. "It wanted you too."

In one swift movement, Kenton swept her body into his powerful arms and carried her into his bedroom, gently easing her onto his bed. He unzipped her dress, and the rest of her clothes came off. He kissed her shoulders, neck, and then her mouth. His rough, calloused hands moved gently down the length of her body, beginning a lust-arousing exploration of her soft flesh.

It was now hardness against softness, man against woman. Briana's body called out his name.

Responding to the seduction of his passion, Briana moaned aloud with shameless pleasure, yielding to her searing need that had been building for months. Briana surrendered completely to his masterful seduction. Their bodies molded in exquisite harmony, gradually increasing until a peak of delight was reached. Then she felt a bolt of thunder race through her body until it exploded into a downpour of fiery sensations. What was happening to her? She'd never felt this heart pounding ecstasy before. In a hot, heady feeling of extreme pleasure, she cried out his name. "Kenton!" She savored the feelings of satisfaction and exhaustion and lay entwined in Kenton's arms. Happiness poured over her mind, body and soul in this sweet moment. At that moment, Briana knew that Kenton was her soul mate. She couldn't imagine loving another man the way she loved Kenton.

The first light of sunrise woke Briana up from a deep sleep. Gazing at Kenton's heaving chest, he looked like a replica of a bronze Adonis with the lower part of his magnificent body hidden beneath the sheet. Dark stubble framed his handsome face. He looked peaceful in his slumber, so Briana decided to surprise him with a gourmet breakfast.

She decided to prepare some of her breakfast selections that she'd planned to offer on her menu. New Orleans barbeque shrimp-n-grits with smoked Gouda cheese, chicken-n-waffles made with buttermilk battered chicken tenders, fried funnel cake, with maple glaze for a topping. As she combed through Kenton's pantry, she found most of the ingredients she would need, and improvised with the rest. An hour later, everything was steaming hot on the island ready to be served.

The surprising aroma of coffee and barbeque woke Kenton up out of a deep sleep. He slipped on his pajama bottoms and walked up to Briana as she put the last touches of her maple glaze on her funnel cakes. He grabbed her from behind kissing her neck. She turned around and gave him a big kiss without getting any glaze on his shoulder. Holding out her finger, she said, "Here, taste this."

Sucking her finger, he moaned. "Mmm. That tastes almost as good as you. You've been getting busy." He looked at the huge breakfast on the island. "What other surprises have you prepared, because I know I smell barbeque?"

Briana pointed to her Barbeque Shrimp-n-Grits.

"Are you going to serve all of this at your restaurant?"

"Yes, but I had to improvise a little today."

"I can't wait."

After feasting on the meal, Kenton took Briana by the hand, leading her back into his bedroom. "Thank you green eyes. I've never feasted on a better breakfast." He gave her a devilish look. "But now, I'm hungry for something else." Climbing back into the bed, he gently pulled her next to him.

Briana exhaled a long sigh of contentment. "Can I ask you a question?"

"What's that baby?"

"Last night I had my first orgasm with you."

He looked her over. Don't tell me you've never experienced one before."

"Nope." Briana laughed. "I know about them, I just never experienced one before. That feeling was wonderful Kenton."

"Come here woman. I can't get enough of you," he said, crushing her into his embrace. He began kissing her slowly. "I'm going to give you a whole bunch of those baby."

Briana felt like a cocoon wrapped in the warmth of his embrace. Kenton slid his hands down slowly, skimming either side of her body to her thighs. His lips pressed against hers gently covering her mouth that tasted as sweet as her funnel cakes.

"Mmm. Nothing tastes better than you, beautiful." He said, burying his face in the softness of her hair.

The sound of his deep sexy voice made Briana's body ache for his tender touch. Kenton removed his pajama bottoms. Briana's body melted against his and her world filled with him. The pleasure of his glorious body felt pure and explosive. Together, they found a tempo that bound their bodies together. Then a moan of ecstasy slipped through Kenton's lips and Briana's body shattered into a galaxy of stars.

Around four, o'clock in the afternoon, the housekeeper came inside to clean the house.

Chapter 14

The award dinner at Edibles restaurant came quickly. Briana chose to wear a bronze shoulder less cocktail dress that ended just above her knees with a matching coat that she'd recently purchased from Neiman Marcus. Wearing her hair up in a cluster of curls, she accessorized her outfit with chocolate diamond jewelry and bronze stilettos. Lillie had taught Briana to dress well when she did attend formal events.

When Briana and Kenton arrived at Edibles, they stood in the doorway of the elegant restaurant for a moment observing well-dressed women wearing expensive evening gowns and men wearing tuxedos and dark suits. Briana's first impression was that all of the smiling faces appeared to be as open and friendly as the Napa Valley landscape. Although Briana's decorating style was casual, she admired the elegant European styling of the restaurant's furnishings, decorated in a dramatic color scheme of tan and black.

Briana saw a tall, slim, distinguished looking, middle-aged man wearing an Armani tuxedo greeting guests at the bottom of the stairs. Standing next to him was a tall, young woman wearing a red satin gown molded to her curvy figure, heavy makeup, and dark brown hair hanging below her shoulders.

Briana made eye contact with the handsome older gentleman. "Kenton, how are you?" Nathaniel greeted.

"Fine." Kenton acknowledged. "Briana, may I introduce Nathaniel Young, the owner of this restaurant, and his daughter Tiffany." Kenton took in a deep breath as he acknowledged Tiffany.

Briana held her hand out to Nathaniel. "Pleased to meet you." She held out her hand to Tiffany, but Tiffany ignored Briana and greeted Kenton.

"I hear you're planning to open a new restaurant," Nathaniel said to Briana, giving her a once over look.

Briana sensed that Nathaniel was fishing for information. Maybe he wanted to find out if her restaurant would be any competition for his.

"Mine is a quaint restaurant, nothing like this." Briana looked around admiring the well-appointed surroundings. Briana's smile faded when Tiffany glared at her. She acknowledged the rude woman with a polite smile.

Briana didn't miss Tiffany rolling her eyes before raising her chin and walking away. Insulted by Tiffany's snub, Briana could see why Kenton broke off their relationship. She could cut Tiffany's contempt with a knife. It was obvious that she still had feelings for Kenton.

"You have to excuse my daughter," Nathaniel apologized. "She complained earlier about a headache," he lied.

Five minutes later, Tiffany walked back toward Kenton and Briana and watched her father hold them hostage while he interrogated Briana. Tiffany spoke to Kenton and ignored Briana again as if Briana was invisible. "Kenton, where have you been hiding? She asked in an angry voice. "I haven't seen you around town lately." Tiffany knew their relationship had ended over two years ago, but she acted as if it had ended yesterday.

"I've been working hard at the winery," Kenton replied stiffly.

As a child, Tiffany was emotionally neglected by Nathaniel. He gave his only child, the apple of his eye, any material thing she wanted. All she wanted was his time, but he never spent any with her. She believed her mother did not love her. After her mother had a mental breakdown, she was institutionalized. Nathaniel hid that from everyone in the Valley. Tiffany tried to compensate for the love she lacked at home by getting her desires for herself. She'd grown into a selfish, narcissist with little regard for the feelings of others.

"I'll break them up if it's the last thing I do," Tiffany said under her breath.

"It's been two years, princess. You need to move on." Nathaniel advised.

"I had to walk away daddy. When I saw her with Kenton, I wanted to scratch her eyes out."

"It's a good thing you didn't do that daughter," Nathaniel said to his heartbroken daughter.

Nathaniel tried to run Briana out of town when he held up her building permit in city hall. He held it up for two reasons. He didn't want the competition from her restaurant. And he wanted to help Tiffany get Kenton back. Running Briana out of town was his last ditch effort to help Tiffany. But his plan backfired. He suspected Kenton had a hand in expediting Briana's building permit. That the Underwood family stood behind Briana's restaurant, gnawed away at Nathaniel's confidence.

He grew up dirt poor in Kansas City, Missouri. At the age of twelve, he made a vow to become a millionaire before he reached twenty-five. Although he'd become a millionaire, with stock investments and businesses, years of extravagant spending, and a bad economy, had caused him to evade paying taxes to the IRS. He'd operated his businesses in the red for several years and kept it a secret.

"My contact in city hall told me that her new restaurant would be in direct competition with Edibles," Nathaniel said. He hid the fact that he was in trouble with the IRS from his daughter. Staring at Briana through unemotional eyes, Nathaniel gulped down the rest of his champagne.

With an upturned chin, Tiffany ignored her father's comment about Briana's restaurant. "She's no competition for me."

Kenton and Briana joined Henrietta and the Underwood employees sitting at a table nearest the podium. Kenton couldn't concentrate on accepting his award tonight. There was too much going on.

First, on the way to his table, he saw Peter Keller and his employees sitting at a table on the other side of the room. He didn't want any beef with Peter tonight. But he remembered his promise to himself about standing up to the man who humiliated his father and antagonized his employees. The devil was busy tonight; Kenton thought.

Second, he was also angered by the way Tiffany treated Briana. He didn't want to deal with any of Tiffany's messiness tonight. She had no problem creating a scene or hurting anyone's feelings in front of anybody who'd pay attention. He was thankful that Briana was nothing like Tiffany.

After an hour had passed, the Master of Ceremonies walked up to the podium, welcomed everyone, and gave a short speech. At the end of his speech, he announced the winner of the award. "And for the winner of this year's Napa Valley Wine Producer of the Year Award, I am proud to announce that Underwood Hills has won based on the brilliant chemical analysis of their Cabernet Sauvignon Reserve. Please come up and accept your award Mr. Underwood."

Kenton walked up to the podium to accept the award and gave his acceptance speech.

Kenton and the Master of Ceremonies shook hands after the ceremony.

When Kenton came back to the table, everyone admired his trophy. After dessert, Briana said, "I'm ready to leave. I want to buy Henrietta a mother's day gift in the morning. I need to get up early to go shopping.

"No problem. Let me use the men's room before we leave. I'll be right back."

When Kenton entered the men's room, he saw Peter Keller standing by the wash bowl drying his hands. Fortunately, no one else was in there. For years, Kenton had kept his feelings inside. But now, he had to confront this bully, the source of his angst. He knew that some people, like Peter, only responded to violence and anger.

Kenton's and Peter's eyes locked. "Kenton, how are you doing?" Peter asked as he dried his hands over the wash bowl.

Kenton felt like a volcano about to erupt. His eyes were icy cold. "I'll tell you how I'm doing Peter. In fact, I'll tell you how I've been doing since I first met you as a twelve year old boy." Kenton balled up his fists as he walked over to face his enemy. "You hurt my father."

"What do you mean I hurt your father?"

"You know what you did. You insulted and humiliated my father in public for years. He was too much of a gentleman to tell you how he felt. But I'm not. You came into my booth at the Mustard Festival upsetting my employees and stealing my customers." Kenton took a step closer to Peter. "I'm telling you this one time buddy. Come near my family, my winery or my employees again—and you're going to be faced with these two ham bones." Kenton held up his fists. "Understand."

"Are you threatening me? You can't do that."

"Try me."

Peter moved to open the door. Kenton bucked causing Peter to jump back.

Kenton stepped aside. "Now get out of here."

Kenton used the men's room, washed his hands, and walked out as if nothing had happened. Kenton had a grin on his face the entire ride home to Sage Creek. He felt like the weight of the world had been lifted from his shoulders. Briana thought he was happy about receiving another award. He didn't mention his face off with Peter to Briana.

Kenton agreed to go shopping with Briana for a Mother's Day gift for Henrietta today. As they walked down Main Street in Walnut Creek, they passed a Tiffany's jewelry store. "Let's go inside here." Kenton said. He knew he wanted to marry Briana, and this was an excellent opportunity for her to select a ring without her knowledge.

"I was thinking of getting Miss Henrietta a nightgown from Neiman Marcus," Briana said.

"Why don't we buy a pendant for Granny and have our names engraved?"

"That sounds like a good idea. What are you going to get your mother?"

"I sent her a card."

"No flowers or candy?" Briana asked.

"Don't get me wrong Briana. I love my mother; we're just not real close. She'll like the card," he said, lifting his palms.

"Why aren't you two close?" Briana asked inquisitively.

Kenton hunched his shoulders but then remembered his promise to be open and honest with Briana. He came out with it. "Because she chose her socialite friends over me, my brothers and my sister when we were growing up. She never put us first. We always came last. Granny was more like a mother to me than my mother." He said with an indifferent attitude.

"Kenton—no. I'm sorry. I didn't know." Briana could see the pain in his eyes. "Do you want to talk about it?"

"No. I don't. Like I said. A card is enough for her."

Briana rubbed Kenton's arm and took his hand.

Kenton and his brothers and sister knew the hard core truth about Jewell Underwood. The only way she would ever become close with any of them was if she were bed ridden and no longer had a social life. She'd only married their father, Joe, to get out of her father's strict household. Though she never said it, her actions spoke for her. She'd never wanted children.

Kenton's thoughts came back to the present, as he remembered why he pulled Briana in front of the jewelry store.

After walking inside, they saw a beautiful platinum heart shaped pendant and decided to have their names engraved. While the attendant engraved their names on the pendant, Kenton walked around the store browsing. He looked at some bridal rings, and asked Briana, which set she preferred.

Briana pointed to a simple one carat round brilliant diamond set in platinum. "That's pretty."

The sales associate asked. "Are you two thinking of getting married?"

Kenton looked at Briana. "I haven't proposed yet."

Briana stepped back from the jewelry case, wondering if Kenton was kidding, or if he had plans to ask her to marry him.

Kenton had planned to confess his love to Briana later on that evening after having dinner with Henrietta.

Briana smiled at the sales associate. "We're only dating right now."

To distract Briana from his intention, Kenton strolled over to a display of men's watches.

Minutes later, the other associate came out with the engraved pendant, showing it to Kenton and Briana. They both approved. "Wrap it up," Kenton said.

When Kenton arrived at Henrietta's, he went to work in his new vineyard. Briana went into the kitchen to prepare a fabulous Mother's Day dinner for Henrietta. Later on that evening, Kenton sat down for dinner with Briana and Henrietta. "Happy Mother's Day, Granny." He gave her a big hug.

Briana handed Henrietta her Mother's Day gift along with a big hug and a card. "Happy Mother's Day, Miss Henrietta."

"Thank you." Henrietta patted them both on the cheeks.

After dinner, Kenton turned to Briana. "Would you spend the night with me again at the ranch? I have to tell you something."

His question piqued her interest. "Okay."

Chapter 15

Kenton wrapped his arm around Briana's shoulders, pouring out his heart as they sat on his sofa. "Briana," he whispered with quiet emphasis. "I told you I had something to ask you."

Briana took in a deep breath and then exhaled to calm her racing heartbeat.

"I want you to know how I feel about you." His eyes clung to her face analyzing her reaction. "You're on my mind twenty-four hours a day." Kenton rubbed his hands against his short hair; his brows lifted in an anxious expression. "I can't stop thinking about you." He lifted her hand to his mouth and kissed it. "I've never felt this way about anyone before."

Briana froze in her seat, closing her mind to what she knew was coming. Sheer fright swept through her as if the world was spinning too quickly.

Rubbing the palm of her hand, Kenton professed. "Briana. I love you."

Briana had promised not to get romantically involved after Duane left. Everyone she'd ever loved had either died or left her. Lowering her head, she exhaled, wondering how she could tell Kenton how she felt.

Kenton watched her pause with curiosity. He looked directly into her eyes. "I want you to see me exclusively, Briana."

Leaning back on the sofa, gripping a pillow, Briana listened to Kenton profess his love. She wasn't surprised to hear him say that. She felt the same way. She turned to face him. "What does love mean to you?"

Kenton noticed her drawl. "What does love mean to me?" He stroked her hand. "I'm not an authority on love, but I do know how I feel about you."

Kenton based his idea of love on emotional feelings. He'd never loved a woman the way he loved Briana.

Briana wished her experience with love could be as simple as Kenton's. She decided to come out with it and tell him what love meant to her. "When it comes to love, I believe I have bad luck." She squeezed the pillow in her lap. "I don't think I'm meant to be in love."

Kenton spoke in his softest voice. "Why do you feel that way, green eyes?"

Briana gave him a heartbreaking look. "Because everyone I've ever loved has either died or left me."

She went on to explain. "First my parents, then my grandfather, and now my grandmother. My entire family is gone." After taking a sip of her wine, she continued. "Even my ex-boyfriend Duane—he left me." With glistening eyes, she confessed, "I am afraid to love you, Kenton. I'm afraid if I do, you will leave me too." Lifting her eyes from the pillow, she turned toward him. "I do love you Kenton, but I'm afraid," she confessed.

Kenton had to agree. Briana was the last living blood relative on her mother's side. "What about your father's side of your family?"

"My grandmother said they didn't care about me."

Kenton remembered his conversation with Granny about them. He loved Briana more because of her raw honesty. He had no idea that the loss of her family had affected like this until now.

How would he be able to develop a deeper relationship with Briana if she felt that way? He had to prove to her that he would never leave her. Sighing deeply, he took the pillow from her lap and pulled her into his arms. He stroked her hair and kissed her face. "Briana, I promise, I will never leave you."

Briana raised her chin and looked up at him through eyes glistening with tears.

Kenton kissed the softness of her cheek. "I'm not going to let you believe that you have bad luck when it comes to love." Lifting her chin, he said. "Every human being is meant to love." Kenton looked her in the eye as he thought about what Granny had told him. "Don't let your relationship with Duane ruin your future happiness."

Briana leaned into Kenton, listening closely to every word he said. She believed his promise never to leave her. She began to feel hopeful and unafraid. Maybe she didn't have bad luck.

"And don't believe you have no more family left. You have your father's side. Maybe you should look into cultivating a relationship with them. You also should expand your definition of family. You have your extended family."

"Yes. I know."

"You have Granny, who is like a mother to you. You also have your best friend Kiara, who is like a sister to you."

"I know. Thanks for reminding me. I've known Miss Henrietta all of my life. She came out to visit my grandmother every year in Baton Rouge when I was a child."

Briana stared into space thinking about her extended family. "I spoke to Kiara the other day on the phone. I told her all about you." Briana's spirits were lifting.

Kenton took her hands again. "Briana, I love you with all of my heart, and I want you to be a part of my family. I don't want you to think you have bad luck. Okay."

"Okay." She decided right then to not be afraid of Kenton leaving.

Noticing the shine on Briana's face, Kenton added. "You are a wonderful woman Briana. You told me that you fed the hungry in New Orleans, and cooked meals at senior centers. You're always doing kind things to help other people Briana. I love you baby."

"I love you too Kenton. Yes. I will see you exclusively."

Kenton held Briana in his arms until she fell asleep. He didn't want to awake her, so he gently slid away from the sofa, placing her head on the pillow. He walked into his library and turned on the light. He sat down on a leather wing chair near the fireplace. He picked up a book he'd been reading by one of his favorite authors, Louis L'Amour. He stared at the cover with a cowboy riding a horse across an open range while he thought about Briana.

Loving Briana and making her happy was more important than anything in the world to Kenton. He'd never confessed his love to a woman before because he'd never truly trusted one until now. He enjoyed making love with Briana and wanted to spend the rest of his life with her. Now that he'd found the love of his life, his deepest feelings freely emerged. He'd opened up and told Briana things he'd never shared with anyone else before.

After sitting in his library for almost two hours, without reading a page, he put his book aside and walked back into the living room. He lifted Briana in his arms and carried her into his bedroom. He lowered her in the center of the bed and removed her clothes. He disrobed, pulled the sheet back, and slid under the covers. He snuggled close to Briana.

Briana stirred and woke up with the movement.

Kenton whispered in her ear, "Are you okay?"

"I'm fine," Briana said, looking into his handsome brown face in the darkness. Kenton's words had been like seeds planted deep into Briana's heart, beginning to sprout.

Kenton kissed her lips. "You fell asleep on the sofa."

Briana returned his kiss. "You should have woke me up."

He ran his hand down the length of her body. "I didn't have the heart."

Briana crossed her leg over his. "You're such a loving person."

"I'll show you real love," he whispered in his deep velvety voice. Pulling her into his embrace, he showered her with kisses all over her body. Briana came fully alive and blissfully happy making love with the man she knew would never leave her.

The next morning, Kenton, woke up a happy man. He'd dreamt about Briana all night. He wanted to do something nice for her because she'd said yes.

Later that afternoon, Kenton, called Rex. "Has Briana mentioned to you that she wants to build a gazebo behind her restaurant?"

"No. I have not discussed that with Briana."

"It must have slipped her mind." He knew she had a lot on her plate with classes and the restaurant. "Can you come up with some gazebo designs? I want to show them to Briana."

"No problem," Rex replied. "I'll have some ready for Briana tomorrow."

The next day, Rex showed Briana three designs. Briana selected one and thanked Kenton for remembering. She hadn't gotten around to that project, because becoming an entrepreneur was more time consuming than she thought. Rex built the gazebo in her poppy field. Briana dedicated it to her mother and the rest of her family.

Chapter 16

Kenton leaned on his elbow watching Briana softly breathing through parted lips. He wished he could spend the entire day in bed making love with her, but he had to leave to check on his new vineyard. He loved spending time with her at Sage Creek. He wondered if she could ever live there. Briana's eyelids fluttered open as if she could read his mind.

"Morning, green eyes."

She sat up and stretched, greeting him. "Good morning."

Sliding his index finger down her cheek, he said. "I love spending time with you here at the ranch."

"I love spending time here too."

"I have a question for you, baby. Do you think you could ever live at Sage Creek?"

Running her fingers through her tangled hair, Briana looked at him through eyes brimming with tenderness and passion. "I can live anywhere as long as you are there."

Kenton's heart filled with happiness. Briana had changed overnight. From her response, he could tell that she no longer believed she had bad luck when it came to love. Now that he had an answer to his question, he changed the subject, because he had a busy schedule today. "So, what do you have planned for today?" He asked.

"After I go to the construction site, I want to look for a bed for my bedroom at Poppy Hill. Know of any good places to buy a bed?"

Stroking his chin, he suggested. "Why don't you go through your interior designer?"

"I don't want my interior designer to shop for my bed. I want to shop for it myself."

Kenton snapped his fingers. "My friend Ricardo owns a showroom downtown. I furnished my ranch with some of his handmade furniture. I'm sure you could find a bed at his showroom." His dark eyebrows arched mischievously.

Since Kenton would be spending a lot of time in her bed, he thought he may as well help her pick one out. The beginning of a smile tipped the corners of his mouth. "I could take some time out of my busy day for you."

"When and where can we meet?" she asked.

"Meet me here around three o'clock and I'll take you to Ricardo's."

"Okay, I'll meet you here at three."

Briana went to check on her construction project after dressing. Kenton left to check on his new vineyard. When Briana arrived at her construction site, she saw that the workers had finished framing the porch and the staircase to the second floor. Walking around the back, she saw the construction workers building a handicapped exit. They'd finished a large redwood trellis outlining the boundaries of a large slate stone patio. Landscapers were planting wisteria to creep up the trellis, and two purple princess trees on each side of the back door. Flowering pink cherry trees had been planted beyond the patio. A large pink stone triple fountain with scalloped edges had been staged near the side of the restaurant out of the way. It would be the center of attraction in the middle of the patio.

After spending the morning watching the workers and talking to the foreman, Briana went back to the ranch to meet Kenton. They drove to Diego Design Studio in downtown Napa.

When they arrived at the studio, Kenton introduced Briana to his friend Ricardo Diego a handsome Ricky Martin look-alike, wearing a white shirt, torn faded blue jeans and cowboy boots. He was the designer of Napa's hottest original handmade furniture. Briana marveled at all of the beautiful handmade and imported furniture. Ricardo gave them a tour of the studio. After browsing for a while, Briana saw a bed that spoke to her. She fell in love with a solid aged bronze wrought iron king size bed with curls, curves and a few straight lines. "This is the bed I want." She whispered to herself.

Kenton had been talking to Ricardo when he heard Briana call out his name. Kenton turned around to see which bed she'd chosen. Suddenly he saw Tiffany standing in the distance, near the back door. Tiffany had followed Kenton to Ricardo's and watched him and Briana walk inside. She'd been following them both around town since the award ceremony. She had no qualms about creating a scene with Kenton anywhere whether it was in front of his business associates, family or friends. Tiffany was determined to break up Kenton's relationship with Briana, because she'd never gotten over him. No skinny woman like Briana was going to steal her man.

Kenton walked up to Briana sitting on the bed.

"What about this bed?" Briana said patting the bed for him to sit down.

Kenton's eyes never left Tiffany's. "Not my taste." He prayed that Tiffany would not create a scene.

Tiffany's eyes never left Kenton's.

Preoccupied with testing the firmness of the mattress, Briana never looked around to see what was going on. "I'm sorry you don't like this one, Kenton, but I think it's beautiful." She didn't care if Kenton didn't like the bed. Gazing into his eyes, she said. "I'm going to buy it." Briana nodded her chin at Ricardo. "Can you have this bed delivered within three weeks?"

"That shouldn't be a problem," Ricardo stated. "Let's go into my office, and we can fill out an invoice."

"I'll follow you," Briana said still sitting, bouncing on the bed.

Kenton watched Tiffany walk toward the bed. Memories of one of her narcissistic incidents came back to haunt him. One night, on a secluded two lane road, they saw a woman stranded on the side of the road. Kenton pulled over to help. Tiffany became angry because she wanted to go home to take a bath. For the woman's sake, Kenton was glad he stopped to help, because not only had her car stopped, but her cell phone battery had died. There was no way for her to call a towing company, so Kenton let her use his cell phone. Tiffany started a heated argument on the way home. Kenton asked Tiffany. "Can't you put yourself in that woman's place? What if that would've been you?"

"The woman could've walked home for all I care," Tiffany replied with a smart mouth.

That was the straw that broke the camel's back. Kenton couldn't tolerate any more of Tiffany's lack of regard for other people. He decided she was not what he was looking for in a wife. Their relationship ended that night after that argument.

Tiffany glared at Briana's back.

Briana saw Kenton's eyes looking away from her. She turned around and saw Tiffany standing by the back door.

Tiffany's eyes left Briana's back and returned to Kenton. Images of his sexy body burned into her mind. No one could make love like Kenton. A raw jealousy crawled up her throat as sour as bile when she thought about Briana making love with her man. Narrowing her eyes at Briana, Tiffany spoke through her teeth. "He's a good lover, isn't he?"

Briana jumped up from the bed. Images of Tiffany's snub at Edibles restaurant came to Briana's memory. Her happy mood veered sharply to displeasure. Briana tried to control her feelings until she noticed Tiffany's hateful glare. She came out with it. "Why are you staring at me?"

Tiffany lashed out in a jealous rage. "I'm not going to let you just take my man."

"Stop it Tiffany, right now!" Kenton snapped.

Straightening her shoulders and clearing her throat, Briana corrected Tiffany's warped accusation. "No one can take your man if he loves you."

Tiffany seethed with mounting rage and delusions that Kenton still loved her.

A shadow of disgust crossed Kenton's face. "Briana, go with Ricardo. I'll handle this."

Dismissing Tiffany, Briana walked away with Ricardo, who held out his elbow. Sliding her hand inside Ricardo's bent arm, Briana gave Kenton a cool smile. "I'll be back when I finish with the invoice."

Kenton stared at Tiffany through fuming eyes. "You just can't help yourself can you. You always have to make a scene. I mean, can't you just leave it alone? That's the second time you've insulted Briana. I'm not going to stand for it anymore."

Through narrow eyes, Tiffany watched Briana walk away with Ricardo. "I haven't begun to insult your little skinny girlfriend. I have more curves than she'll ever have, and you've known me since seventh grade. What does she have that I don't have?"

"How about a kind and loving heart? Those are two things you know nothing about." His voice hardened. "And she's not trying to corner me into marriage or turn me into something I'm not."

"How can you say that to me?" She removed a tissue from her handbag. "I have shown you nothing but love, Kenton," she said, dabbing at the corners of her dry eyes. She stepped closer to him. "I planned trips all around the world for us when we dated. I entertained your customers at my luxurious home. I tried to get you out of that rusty ranch. I hired the best caterers and threw extravagant cocktail parties for you. How can you say I don't have a loving heart?"

Kenton stiffened as he glared at Tiffany. "All of it Tiffany was for you! You only love yourself. I never wanted to live your glitzy lifestyle. Yes, I love my rusty ranch. If you had taken the time to get to know me, you would've found out that I enjoy living a simple lifestyle. All of your bling, glamour and extravagant living, that's all about you Tiffany! That's not the way I roll. Never have. Never will."

Tiffany stood in front of Kenton's face whining. "But, Kenton, Don't you love me anymore?"

"It's been over for two years Tiffany! Move on with your life."

With protruding eyes, Tiffany whirled around and said through clenched teeth, "It's not over until I say it's over!" Rushing out of the front door, she shattered a display of Native American pottery on the way.

Briana walked out of Ricardo's office holding her invoice as she saw Tiffany rushing through the front door. She walked back toward Kenton. "You need to get a restraining order against Tiffany. I think she's stalking you. How did she know you'd be here?"

"Yeah, maybe so." Kenton stood there fuming and huffing through widened nostrils. "The woman is crazy."

In Briana's opinion, Tiffany was crazy like a fox. She knew what she was doing. No one insulted people by accident. Briana figured Tiffany must feel threatened in some way because every time they met, Tiffany had no problem batting out insults. How could Tiffany think Briana was stealing her man? Hopefully,

Kenton would find some way to deal with Tiffany's jealousy because Briana couldn't tolerate any more of her insults. Briana thought Tiffany was a loose cannon, liable to do anything.

After watching Tiffany's jealous rage, Briana shook her head out of a mixture of pity and disgust. She couldn't imagine forcing herself on a man who didn't want her. Why did Tiffany still want Kenton? Maybe she had a low self-esteem. It was obvious Tiffany was still in love with Kenton and couldn't let go.

Before leaving the showroom, Kenton insisted on paying Ricardo for the broken pottery. They left Ricardo's and spent the rest of the day at Sage Creek.

Briana's experience with Tiffany caused her to sit silently in the passenger seat on the ride to Sage Creek. She was angrier than anything, because once again, she'd been hurt by Tiffany's words. She couldn't imagine Kenton seriously dating a woman like Tiffany. Their relationship was a testament to his bad decision making. She wondered if he made bad decisions in other areas of his life. When they arrived at the ranch, Kenton opened the door, but Briana remained in the car.

"What's wrong?" Kenton stuck his head in the open car door.

"I don't understand why you dated a woman as crazy as Tiffany."

He hunched his shoulders. "It was a bad decision."

"It makes me wonder if you make bad decisions in other areas of your life."

"What's the matter? Are you angry that Tiffany and I had a fight, or do you really care about my decision-making abilities?"

"I'm concerned about your decision-making capabilities," Briana said in misdirected anger. She was actually angry at Tiffany.

"You sound bossy and controlling."

"Bossy and controlling. Where did that come from?"

"I wanted to have a talk with you about your hard-headed bossy ways Briana. I just haven't had the chance."

"Hard-headed, bossy?"

"Yes."

"When have I been bossy?"

"An example comes fresh to my mind." He sat back down in the car. "Remember when you criticized my award wall?"

"Yes."

"It takes a bossy person to criticize someone's accomplishments."

"If you remember, I wasn't criticizing your accomplishments. I just said that the wall reflects a lot about your personality. Like being competitive and ambitious."

"Briana, I do not like bossy people, let alone bossy women."

"So now you're a male chauvinist?"

"I'm far from being a chauvinist. I just don't like to be controlled or told what to do."

"I didn't tell you what to do with that wall?"

"No, you didn't, but you got me to think about taking my awards down indirectly. That's controlling."

"I didn't mean anything. You can keep your awards up if you want."

"That's what I mean. You don't have the right to tell me what to do with that wall. I'm a grown man, and I'm not used to any woman telling me what to do."

"Okay. I acknowledge that I can be a bit bossy."

"Good," Kenton said. "Let's acknowledge our differences. Can you agree that you're bossy, and I'm competitive?"

"Yes. I can. I guess we need to find a decent way to argue over our different personalities."

"That sounds like a good idea," Kenton said.

"Are you prepared to put up with my hard-headed bossy ways?" Briana asked.

"Only if you're prepared to put up with my competitive behavior." Kenton smiled taking Briana's hand. "I know we are only dating, but I'm committed to you Briana. There are going to be things we disagree about, but I love you enough to work those problems out."

"I'm also committed to you Kenton. I love you enough to work our problems out."

"Good. So does that mean we can go into the house? I'm hungry."

Briana laughed. "Okay. We're both different, but we love each other."

The next day, Briana woke up early, prepared breakfast and drove over to the construction site. She was amazed to see how quickly the men worked. They were beginning to hang drywall on the frames for the private banquet rooms. Rex walked upstairs to the second floor to give Briana a tour of her living quarters. After Rex had finished with the tour, Briana sat in her bedroom window seat fantasizing about how her life had changed since relocating to Napa. She would soon be an entrepreneur instead of an unemployed chef. Gazing through the window, she looked at the tip of the Douglas fir tree and felt that warm connection with her mother.

As weeks had passed, Briana and Kenton made love every chance they got. As time passed, Briana felt a deep emotional intensity in their lovemaking.

As the completion date came closer, Briana's excitement grew. She couldn't wait until they finished her restaurant. The last time she went to the construction site she noticed Rex and the workers applying finishing touches of paint to the interior walls. They had just finished installing her beautiful hardwood floors and gourmet kitchen appliances.

This morning, Briana had prepared a surprise luncheon, in Henrietta's kitchen, for Rex and his crew. She wanted to thank them for completing her restaurant on schedule. She saw Rex as she pulled up to the restaurant with her car filled with food.

"Rex, I've prepared a luncheon for you and the men, to celebrate the completion of my restaurant."

Rex and the hungry group of men made a makeshift table next to the Douglas fir tree.

Briana set the table with disposable paper plates and utensils. She brought out Po-Boy sandwiches filled with fried shrimp, coleslaw, barbeque sauce, lettuce, tomato, and spicy pickles. She also prepared a seafood pasta dish in a tomato based sauce with mussels, shrimp and crab. After she had set all of the food out, she said loudly. "Come and get it."

Rex and the hungry group of men scarfed everything down within minutes. She recalled Kenton insinuating that the Bay Area's population might not care for Low Country cooking. She laughed when she saw the empty plates. She was pleased to see that her Low Country cuisine satisfied the palate of Rex and his construction workers.

Later that night Briana sat at her computer finishing a late report for one of her online classes. She'd finally completed all of her courses, earning an "A" in each class.

Chapter 17

The eight thousand square foot, two-story, pale yellow structure, featured a white veranda that wrapped around the entire building on both floors. Briana's eyes shimmered as she and Kenton gazed at the sign hanging from the eaves of the building displaying Poppy Hill Restaurant in orange letters. Palm trees swayed in oversized pots, positioned on either side of the large porch. White wooden rocking chairs had been spaced out on each side of the door.

Every window inside had views of rolling hills covered with vineyards. Floor to ceiling windows welcomed natural sunlight into the large foyer. Dark hardwood floors led to the granite reservation desk at the base of the curved wrought iron staircase that extended upward to Briana's living quarters on the second floor.

Kenton followed Briana carrying two champagne glasses with a bottle of Dom Perignon champagne. His plan was to toast each room. He hadn't seen the finished version of the building yet. Placing the glasses on the black granite reservation desk, he twisted the cork. Champagne burst out of the bottle spilling onto the counter prompting Briana to jump back and laugh with excitement. Kenton quickly filled the champagne glasses and handed one to Briana. He was proud of Briana. He remembered when she told him that she wanted to accomplish something important in life. Well, she'd done it. She'd accomplished something important in life, and it was her dream. Raising his chin, he thrust out his chest giving Briana an admirable look. "Congratulations Briana. You did it."

Briana stood tall, feeling relief as if she'd conquered the world. Becoming an entrepreneur was harder than she thought, but she'd done it. Now all she had to do was run her restaurant successfully. Unable to contain her excitement, she responded to Kenton's compliment. "I can't believe my restaurant was once only a dream. Let me show you around," she said as she took a sip of her champagne.

She led Kenton into the large comfortable lounge area with a full bar featuring a floor to ceiling fireplace. Chocolate and caramel colored leather club chairs in groups of three or four were scattered throughout the lounge that could be converted into a dining room to accommodate large parties. They walked into the spectacular main dining room featuring a large fresco of the Napa Valley. It covered the entire south wall. Dark wood dining tables with brown leather chairs provided seating for dinner guests. The pale gray walls provided a soft backdrop for the artwork. The dining room furnishings provided a stage worthy of her unique cuisine.

Kenton made a toast to Briana. "May this room seat many of your happy, contented customers fortunate to dine on your cooking."

Lifting her glass, Briana took another sip of champagne. She added to Kenton's toast. "May this room be forever filled with large gatherings of family, friends and guests."

Kenton took a sip of champagne and winked at Briana. "To large family gatherings."

On the first floor, Briana's office was located in the east wing. A large gourmet kitchen took up the entire rear of the restaurant. The west wing held three large private banquet rooms, all decorated in colors of wildflowers. There was the all-white Desert Lily Room, the yellow and white Narcissus Room, and a Chocolate Lily Room.

Briana made the entire three thousand square foot second floor her living quarters. After toasting all of the upstairs living quarters, they ended up in Briana's pale peach bedroom suite decorated in varying shades of orange, yellow and white. Multicolored velvet pillows accented the headboard, and a poppy hued velvet bench sat at the foot of her bed. Plantation shutters graced all of the large windows. Each had spectacular views of surrounding vineyards and the Napa River.

Briana twirled around. "This is my room." Walking over to the window next to her bed, she gazed at her beloved Douglas fir tree. After falling onto the window seat, she patted the velvet cushion, offering Kenton, a seat next to her. It had been hard keeping her bedroom suite hidden from Kenton until she finished decorating. She'd commissioned photo art of her poppy field and hung them in frames on the walls. Standing up, she continued to twirl around in her bedroom. Walking over to her bed, she slid her hand across the headboard. "Remember this?"

Kenton admired the aged bronze finish of her wrought iron bed she'd purchased from Ricardo's. It looked good in her bedroom. He outlined the curls and curves on the headboard with his hand, then pressed his fingers on the mattress to test its softness. His eyebrows arched mischievously. "It feels comfortable." The warmth of his smile echoed in his voice. "This building personifies you Briana."

Tilting her head, Briana asked. "What do you mean?"

"It's casual yet beautiful. Just like you. I like that." He said scanning her body.

Briana beamed with happiness.

Kenton had thoughts of making love to Briana to celebrate, but then his mind focused on how he would propose to her. With plans on buying a ring tomorrow, he wondered where he would propose to her and where they would go for their honeymoon. Pausing for a moment, he couldn't remember ever asking Briana how she felt about traveling. Looking into her eyes, he queried. "I have a question for you green eyes?" Sitting down on the edge of the bed, he asked. "Have you ever traveled outside of the country?"

Briana walked over to him and stood between his legs. Massaging the sides of his unshaven jaws, she replied. "No. I've never traveled outside of the country. I'm not big on airplanes, but I'll fly if I need to go somewhere."

"Which foreign country would you like to visit?"

Scratching her chin, Briana looked deep into his eyes and said. "Rome, Italy."

He took her hands into his. "What intrigues you about Rome baby?" His gaze was as soft as a caress.

Briana ran her fingers through his short, thick hair. "I've seen interesting programs on television about Rome." Her head was spinning from the champagne.

Giving Briana a mischievous look, Kenton rubbed her hands. He felt immense pleasure at her closeness and touching. "I think of Rome as a romantic city."

His deep, sensual voice sent a ripple of awareness through Briana's body.

Pulling her closer to him, Kenton looked her over seductively. Leaning his face against her torso, he said, "Maybe we'll visit Rome one day."

Pulling her down onto the bed next to him, he kissed her neck, then her breasts then her mouth. The caress of his lips on her mouth set her body aflame. His lips continued to explore her soft honey hued flesh. He unbuttoned her blouse and the flames of passion burned within his core.

Kenton's rough vintner's hands felt so good to Briana. Aroused now, she drew herself closer to him. She felt his hands move magically over her breasts. She moaned aloud with erotic pleasure as she surrendered her body over to his masterful seduction. At the end of their lovemaking, she savored the feeling of happiness Kenton left with her. They both lay entwined until sleep crept upon them.

The next morning, Kenton, left early. He kissed Briana and said. "I'm in a hurry baby. I need to run some errands today. I won't be able to meet you for lunch." Kenton was confident that he wanted to marry Briana. He drove straight to Tiffany's jewelry store in Walnut Creek. He saw the same attractive brunette sales associate who showed him the rings.

"I remember you." She gave him a friendly toothy smile. "You were in here the other day with your girlfriend. She's beautiful." She complemented.

"Thank you," Kenton said as he moved closer to the case with the ring. "I'd like to see the ring my girlfriend admired on Mother's Day."

She pulled out the ring.

He inspected the same one carat round brilliant diamond in a platinum setting. "Does this ring come in a larger stone?"

"Yes it does."

Kenton realized that Briana had understated taste. He knew not to get a stone too large. "Can you put a two-carat stone in this setting?"

"Here is a two carat solitaire in the same setting?"

"I'll take it. Wrap it up." He purchased the entire bridal set for himself and Briana. He held out his chest thinking about the achievement oriented, independent, Low Country cooking woman that he loved.

Kenton thought about proposing to Briana in her beloved poppy field. When he returned to Henrietta's, he went straight to his room to hide the ring. After checking on the winery, he went over to the restaurant to check on Briana.

Briana had been busy running around organizing and stocking the kitchen with dry goods and spices.

Kenton stopped Briana in her tracks on her way to the kitchen. Taking her by the hand, he asked. "Want to go on a picnic tomorrow in your poppy field?" He'd planned to propose to her in her gazebo.

An energized Briana rushed her words. "A picnic. You must be kidding. I don't have time for that. I have to hire employees and prepare for my grand opening."

Kenton saw the excitement in her sparkling eyes. "Come on, it's only lunch. We both have to eat."

"Your flattery is not going to work, Kenton."

Kenton knew Briana had a ton of work to do. Then he realized her birthday was next week. "Okay, are you going to celebrate your birthday next week?"

"I forgot all about my birthday. You have any ideas?"

Going to her gazebo wouldn't be much of a birthday celebration, he thought, so he asked her. "Why don't we celebrate your birthday in the city? Let me take you out dancing in San Francisco."

"That sounds great." She said giving Kenton an easy nod.

"Okay. It's a date." Kenton decided to propose in San Francisco.

Kenton had Jimmie drive the limousine to Crustacean's a five star seafood restaurant on Maiden Lane in San Francisco to celebrate Briana's birthday. After dinner, they danced the night away at a private club in the famous Palace Hotel, downtown San Francisco. After finding an empty table, Kenton pulled out an upholstered chair for Briana. "I'll be right back."

Briana pushed herself up from the table to find the ladies' room. She listened to the slow hypnotic music played by a live band on the way.

Kenton walked over to the maître d and handed him a folded one hundred dollar bill. He asked if the band could play Briana's favorite song, Ordinary People by John Legend. The maître d agreed. Kenton walked back to his table to wait for Briana. His love for Briana was urgent. Feeling a little nervous, he felt his coat pocket for the ring box. More than anything, he wanted to spend the rest of his life with Briana, the only woman he'd ever loved inside and out in his twenty-nine years of life.

When Briana returned, Kenton's eyes brimmed with tenderness and passion. He held out his hand to her. "They're playing your song, green eyes. Want to dance?"

Briana gave him a skeptical look while walking into his arms. "Did you ask the band to play that song?"

Kenton gave her a devilish smile as he held her close. In the middle of the song, Kenton stopped dancing.

Briana gave him a curious look. "What's wrong?"

Kenton gave Briana a seductive look. He reached into his coat pocket and pulled out a little aqua box. He kneeled on one knee. He opened the box and took out the ring.

Gasps could be heard all across the dance floor when people saw him kneel down on one knee.

Gently raising Briana's hand to his mouth, Kenton kissed it. "Briana. Will you marry me?"

Shocked, Briana looked around at the whispering audience and the people on the dance floor. Kenton's proposal was completely unexpected. She was supposed to be celebrating her birthday. She became instantly wide awake. Her heart sang with delight. With glistening eyes, she replied. "Yes, Kenton. I will marry you."

The band had stopped playing. Everyone on the dance floor began clapping when they saw Kenton put the ring on her left hand and third finger.

Kenton stood up and took Briana into his embrace and gave her a slow drugging kiss. The people on the dance floor began clapping again.

After the long kiss, Briana began to feel moisture on her legs. Looking down, she saw that Kenton's pant leg was soaking wet at the knee. He had kneeled down on a spilled drink. She pointed it out to him. Kenton threw back his head and let out a great sound of laughter. Briana joined in on the laugh as they walked off the dance floor holding hands, feeling a warm glow of happiness.

Forty-five minutes later they walked hand in hand down Market Street. They met Jimmy talking on his cell phone in the limousine. Kenton opened the back door for Briana. "Let's go Jimmie."

Leaning her head against Kenton's shoulder, Briana gave him a seductive kiss on the ride to Poppy Hill.

The next morning, Kenton, leaned back in the bed looking at Briana. Rolling her head on a pillow, Briana opened her eyes to see Kenton's handsome face.

"Morning, beautiful."

"Good morning, handsome."

Leaning on one elbow, he drew his index finger across her eyebrow. "Did you sleep well?"

Stretching out her arms, she yawned. "Yeah. I dreamt about us."

Still smiling, he grabbed a curly spindle in Briana's huge wrought iron headboard. "Tell me."

Briana held out her left hand, her eyes twinkled at the engagement ring. "It's beautiful."

"I almost chose the smaller stone, but I wanted you to have this one. What do you think? Too big?"

"It's perfect. I love it."

Contented with her answer, Kenton asked. "So what were you dreaming about?"

"I dreamt that we were both exhausted all of the time because you worked hard at the winery, and I worked hard at the restaurant. Do you think we bit off more than we can chew?"

Kenton took her face into his hands, holding it gently. "That's a good problem with an easy solution."

Briana gave him a curious look, waiting to hear his solution.

"I can always get Vanessa to take over the day to day operations of the winery and you can always hire a general manager to run your restaurant. Don't worry baby. We're going to have a great life together. We'll see the world."

Although Briana loved Kenton's vision of traveling the world, she didn't want to be one of those couples who lived out of a suitcase. She wanted to spend more time at home where she could live and work in her restaurant. Maybe she would occasionally travel. But they would need to discuss their travel plans a bit more. For now everything was fine with her.

After observing the apprehension on Briana's face. Kenton remembered that she'd never traveled outside the country. "I promise. We won't travel that much." He reassured her by pulling her into his embrace.

Briana felt comforted with Kenton's promise. "Okay."

"Hey, you want to ride with me out to the ranch today?"

"Shouldn't we tell Miss Henrietta about our engagement today?"

"You're right Briana we should tell Granny today." Kenton decided to tell the rest of his family next week. He quickly turned his attention back to Briana. You know Granny is going to want you to stop calling her Miss Henrietta."

"You think so?"

Kenton nodded his head.

"I see you call her Granny. I used to call my grandmother Nana."

"Why don't you call her Granny-Nana?" Kenton said laughing at his joke.

Briana burst out laughing. Happiness and contentment glimmered in her eyes because now she had a family. She was no longer alone in the world, and she couldn't wait to meet his siblings.

"I have an idea. How about we throw Granny-Nana a birthday party at Poppy Hill."

"I think she'd love that," Kenton said.

"Come on, we better tell Granny-Nana the good news."

A week had passed since they'd given Henrietta the news about the engagement. Kenton had also called his brothers and sister and his mother in Los Angeles. Henrietta asked when they planned to marry. Briana told her that she always wanted to get married in the spring. Kenton said any time of the year was good for him.

Chapter 18

It was the end of May and time was moving quickly. Briana's highest priority was to prepare for her grand opening. After advertising her job openings in local media, she'd received resumes for each position and made selections. For her general manager, she hired Trevor Howard, a twenty-four year old, physically fit, dark brown man with an agreeable disposition. He'd just graduated from Sonoma State University with a degree in hospitality management. She also hired a front desk reservation's clerk, an accounting clerk, and a part-time bookkeeper. She signed up with a CPA firm, and hired Kenton's brother, Justin as her lawyer. As her sous-chef, she hired Jacques Laguerre, a French national, who she would personally teach how to prepare Low Country cuisine. She also hired three cooks, five waiters, three bus boys, a dishwasher, and a janitor. To help with large events, she hired a large catering company on retainer. She'd also sent for her grandmother's cook, Mrs. Mack. There was no way Briana could serve Low Country cuisine without the help of Mrs. Mack.

Today, Briana needed to pick up Mrs. Mack from the airport. She couldn't miss her standing at the Delta Airlines baggage claim wearing a tailored suit and heels. Mrs. Mary Louise Mack was a petite, dark skinned woman in her late sixties with a kind face and heart to match. Standing at five foot four, she always kept her weight down and wore just a touch of makeup. Briana waved at Mrs. Mack through the window. She waved back, greeting Briana with a pretty smile.

Briana pulled over to the passenger loading zone and popped her trunk. Mrs. Mack tipped the middle-aged skycap who happily brought her baggage over to Briana's car. After hugging each other for what seemed like an eternity, Briana and Mrs. Mack stood by the car catching up on their lives while the skycap loaded the luggage. Briana felt nothing but fondness and love for Mrs. Mack, who helped raise her from a toddler. She was her grandmother's longtime cook, nanny and housekeeper and like a second grandmother to Briana.

Briana wiped her glistening eyes. "Miss Mack, how are you?" She only called her Miss Mack when they were alone otherwise she called her Mrs. Mack in front of other people.

Mrs. Mack wiped her sixty-seven-year-old tear stained eyes with a dainty white handkerchief, embroidered with pink flowers. "I'm fine honey. I miss you."

"I miss you too Miss Mack. I have so much to tell you. Here, let me help you get into the car."

Mrs. Mack stepped up into Briana's SUV. "I have a lot to tell you about your grandmother's house."

Briana quickly stepped into her SUV and started the ignition. "Tell me in the car. We have to get out of here, or they'll give me a ticket," she paused, smiling.

Mrs. Mack scanned Briana. "My, my, my. Don't you look good? You just came out here and changed your life."

"It's been wonderful since I've been here. I renovated Nana's old cottage into my restaurant, and my boyfriend Kenton has asked me to marry him."

"Wait a minute. Did you just say you're getting married?"

Briana nodded, holding out her hand so Mrs. Mack could see her ring. Briana had told Mrs. Mack that she was opening a restaurant, but she hadn't had a chance to tell her she was getting married.

"Tell me about him and your restaurant.

Briana told her all about Kenton and Poppy Hill.

"I'm happy for you." Mrs. Mack wiped the corner of her eyes with her handkerchief.

"Tell me how everything is going back home since I left?"

"All the workers are still excited about receiving the money your grandmother left them. No one expected that." She gave Briana a concerned look. "Nashae is gone."

Briana raised her brows as she drove. "Oh," Briana paused. "Where did she go?"

"Remember your grandmother stipulated in her will that Nashae couldn't receive her money unless she enrolled in college. Well, Nashae enrolled into Xavier University. She's majoring in Sociology. She and Roscoe had a falling out over her money. Roscoe thought his daughter had enrolled only to receive your grandmother's money. Roscoe feared that once Nashae ran through the money she'd come running back home for her old job."

"What about the others?"

"Roscoe is still working as the butler. Even though, there's not much for him to do, he still tries to boss me around, but I tell him where to go. He saved his twenty-five thousand dollars for retirement."

"Who's helping you with the cleaning now that Nashae is gone?" Briana asked.

"With you and Lillie gone, there's nobody to clean up after other than Roscoe, so I handle most of the household chores by myself. I keep everything pretty much cleaned and dusted."

"What about the grounds, how do they look?" Briana queried.

"The same. Ezekiel and his nephew take good care of the grounds. Ezekiel bought a new truck and some landscaping equipment with his money."

Briana nodded as she listened.

"Between me, Roscoe and Ezekiel, we keep everything together at the house." Mrs. Mack paused for a moment. "Are you planning to sell the house now that you're living out here?"

"Are you kidding, I can't do that. That's where I grew up. I want to keep Nana's house for my future children. I'll probably come there every summer. I'd love it if you, Roscoe and Ezekial remained there."

Mrs. Mack beamed with joy after hearing Briana's decision. "I can't wait to see your new restaurant."

"We'll arrive at the restaurant any minute now, but before we get there, I need to tell you something Miss Mack. I want you to teach all of the cooks how to prepare Low Country cuisine."

"Honey I'd be happy to do that."

After driving for thirty minutes, Briana pulled up in front of her restaurant. "This is it."

Mrs. Mack's eyes widened when she saw the beautiful pale yellow two story structure. Turning to face Briana, she gasped. "Briana. Look what you did." She admired the sign that hung from the eves. "Poppy Hill Restaurant." She grinned, "I like the name."

"Come on in. I live upstairs. I'll take you to the guest bedroom so you can rest a while." Briana said.

Trevor came out quickly to help Briana with Mrs. Mack's bags. Briana took Mrs. Mack by the arm as they walked inside. Camille, the reservation's clerk greeted them with a big smile.

Briana introduced everyone. "Trevor, Camille, this is Mrs. Mack, my good friend. She'll be training the cooks."

"Hello, Mrs. Mack," Camille said.

Trevor smiled politely. "It's a pleasure to meet you Mrs. Mack."

Mrs. Mack smiled at them both. She gave Briana a nod of approval for their professionalism.

Trevor took Mrs. Mack's bags to the guest bedroom on the second floor. Meanwhile, Briana gave Mrs. Mack a quick tour of the restaurant paying close attention to the gourmet kitchen and private banquet rooms.

Mrs. Mack marveled at Briana's style and creativity. "This looks like you Briana." Tears welled in her eyes. "I'm so proud of you. Your grandmother would be proud too."

After the tour, Briana walked Mrs. Mack up to her room. Before leaving, Briana said, "If you get hungry come downstairs. I made some gumbo."

It had been a week since Briana hired her staff. She provided them with peach polo shirts with the Poppy Hill logo embroidered near the shoulder and tan chinos as uniforms. For the next three weeks, Mrs. Mack trained the kitchen cooks on how to prepare Low Country cuisine while Briana trained Jacques.

Trevor sent announcements to the local media to advertise the restaurant's grand opening. He included the names of local celebrities who would be in attendance.

Briana hired local musicians to perform at the grand opening. Later in the week, Briana had planned to have a staff meeting to fine tune the details for the grand opening.

At the staff meeting, Briana informed everyone that she'd set August fifteenth as the date for the grand opening. After announcing that she was expecting three hundred guests, everyone sighed with relief when she informed them that she'd hired a catering company to help with the extra work. Everyone was expected to be on time, and on duty, dressed in their uniforms. After going over the menu, Briana asked them all to taste and memorize each menu item.

Today, Briana had planned to teach Jacques how to prepare seafood gumbo. She still couldn't believe that the French national didn't know how to prepare gumbo, the staple soup of New Orleans. She knew it would be a bestseller just like it was at 'M' bistro.

After giving him a print out of her recipe, she stood over him while he sautéed bell pepper, onion, celery and garlic in olive oil. Ten minutes later, she said. "It's time for you to transfer the vegetables to a bowl."

Jacques quickly transferred the vegetables to a bowl.

"Now to make a rue, you need to turn up the heat and brown your flour."

"Ah, brown gravy. That's easy." Jacques stated with his heavy French accent.

Briana recited a list of important ingredients to add to his rue: chopped red peppers, bay leaves, salt and pepper, chicken, sausage, shrimp, crab, other seafood and finally Gumbo file.

Grateful for teaching him how to prepare the soup, he thanked Briana.

"We'll probably need to prepare gumbo every day after we open," Briana said.

Jacques ladled Gumbo into a bowl and tasted it. "It's delicious," he said, then continued eating.

Mrs. Mack walked into the kitchen wearing her uniform. She'd come ready to teach the cooks how to prepare Lillie's greens and cornbread which would also become a daily staple on Briana's menu.

"Good afternoon Briana," Mrs. Mack greeted.

"Hey, Mrs. Mack, how are you feeling today?"

"I'm fine." She didn't bother complaining about her aches and pains. Pulling a batch of prewashed mustard greens from the refrigerator, she transferred them into a large pot. "Smells like you're making gumbo."

"I just trained Jacques how to prepare it." Walking over to the stove, Briana took a peek at the bubbling soup. Jacques and the other cooks were enjoying bowls of the soup. They were all learning quickly how to prepare and enjoy Low Country cuisine. Briana couldn't wait for her grand opening.

Chapter 19

Kenton eagerly opened an envelope that had been hidden under a stack of Henrietta's mail for over a month. It was from the International Wine and Spirit Competition. The letter indicated that he'd won the competition in the Americas and Caribbean Spirits Producer category. He won based on his wine's chemical and microbiological analysis. After reading the letter, Kenton bounced from foot to foot, doing his football touchdown dance, excited that Underwood Hills had won the coveted competition. He wanted to shout out as loud as he could about winning which would offer international recognition to more than a billion customers. The letter included an airline ticket for him to receive his award on August fifteenth. Kenton's eyes froze wide open after reading the letter again. The award-ceremony was on the same day as Briana's grand opening!

Kenton hesitated as he realized his dilemma. On the one hand, he fantasized about receiving the prestigious award. On the other hand, he wanted to attend Briana's grand opening. He wished he could change Briana's grand opening date, but after analyzing all of the alternatives, he realized her date was set in stone. He knew Briana would hate him if he did not attend her event.

He wanted to go because, receiving this award meant Underwood Hills would receive international exposure to over a billion customers, but he didn't want to let Briana down.

Several days had passed since Kenton had found the letter. He'd decided to go to Italy. He didn't want to jeopardize his relationship with Briana by telling her he couldn't attend her grand opening. She'd worked hard to start her business. He knew she felt a deep emotional attachment to her restaurant. How could he break the news to her? He couldn't come up with an easy way to tell Briana.

Late one night, after the restaurant closed, Kenton sat in Briana's dining room with his back to the fresco. He smiled when Briana brought out dinner.

Briana brought him one of her specials. "I hope you enjoy this meal."

Kenton looked up at her with guilty eyes. "I have something to tell you Briana."

"What's that?" Briana gave him a perplexed look.

Kenton came out with it. "I won the International Wine and Spirit Competition, the one I told you about. I'm supposed to receive an award in Italy on August fifteenth. But that's the same day as your grand opening." He exhaled deeply, then waited for her response. His voice softened. "I can't be in both places at the same time baby."

After Briana had absorbed his statement, the light dimmed in her olive green eyes. Kenton had been instrumental in helping her start her restaurant, and she wanted him to attend her grand opening. But she also understood how much this award meant to him

"I know how important this award is to you Kenton." She said softly. "I'll be a little disappointed. But I'll understand if you choose not to attend my grand opening."

Kenton lowered his gaze. "I'm doing this to get international exposure to over a billion new customers."

"A billion new customers. Wow." Briana stated. She wanted him to increase sales and prestige for the winery. She thought deeper about his dilemma and asked. "If you don't accept the award, won't you still get the exposure to the billion customers?"

Kenton remained quiet for a moment contemplating her question. "Yes, I will. The competition generates free media coverage to over one and a half billion people worldwide."

"Then why do you want to go, if you can still get the free media coverage?"

Kenton didn't know how to answer that question. He didn't know why he wanted to go. He only knew that something deep inside of him yearned to receive that award. He began to feel guilty because of his impossible dilemma.

No matter how badly Briana wished Kenton would come to her grand opening, she would never force him to do anything he didn't want to do. She wanted him to do whatever was in his heart. She would support his decision.

Kenton shook his head regretfully, his eyes speaking for him. He paused for a moment and said, "I choose to go to Italy."

Briana accepted his decision as the desire of his heart. Feeling drained, from a long day's work and their intense discourse, Briana left Kenton in the dining room and walked up the staircase. Halfway up she turned around and stared into blank space. "I'm going to bed, Kenton."

Kenton pushed himself away from the table as he watched her walk up the stairs. "Do you want me to spend the night?"

Still staring into space, she said. "Do whatever you want, Kenton." She continued to walk up the stairs.

Lowering his head, Kenton walked out of the front door. "I'll spend the night at the ranch." He didn't blame Briana for feeling disappointed.

Kenton felt guilty all the way to his ranch. Once there, he shifted around in his library chair nervously rubbing the back of his neck and rubbing his knees.

Why couldn't he find any peace? He asked himself hard questions. Did he really need to accept that award? He thought about Briana's question. Wouldn't he still get exposure to the billion customers whether he went to Italy or not? His answer was yes. He would. He asked himself the hardest question of all. Was Briana's happiness more important than receiving another award? His answer was yes. His love for Briana was more important than anything, even accepting another award anywhere. Kenton acknowledged that he could receive a wine award any time. But crossing paths with a woman like Briana only came once in a lifetime. He wasn't willing to take the chance of losing Briana over a wine-award or even a billion customers.

Right then and there, he chose to attend Briana's grand opening. He picked up the telephone and called the airlines. He changed the name on the airline ticket to Vanessa Jimenez. He would send her to receive the award for Underwood Hills Winery.

Later that night Briana lay in her bed disappointed about Kenton choosing to receive another award over attending her grand opening. His choice made her feel like he thought no more of her than a bottle of wine. Now that she realized her place in his heart, she buried her feelings and went to sleep.

The next morning Kenton went to the winery tasting room. He greeted Vanessa behind the bar washing wine glasses. Staring at the twelve foot wall from the bar, he thought about Briana. All of those plaques did cover the entire twelve foot wall. Now that he saw them from a different perspective, the wall looked cluttered. He whispered under his breath. "Dad I'll keep some of your awards in a safe place for our family, but for now, some of them have got to come down." He went to the utility closet and pulled out a metal ladder.

When he returned, he looked at Vanessa stacking clean wine glasses under the counter and asked. "Vanessa, how would you like to take a trip to Europe?"

Vanessa stood up straight staring at him. "A trip to Europe?"

"Yes, maybe you could take one of your brothers too."

Speaking in her happiest voice, she said. "Mr. Underwood that sounds like a dream come true. I've never been to Europe. Are you sure I can take one of my brothers?"

"Yes." He pulled out the airline ticket from his back pocket and handed it to Vanessa. "Here. I changed this ticket into your name. I'll get one for the brother you want to take."

Vanessa stared at him like she was in the middle of a dream. "Mr. Underwood that is so nice of you." Opening up the ticket jacket, she saw that the flight was for Tuscany, Italy. Her eyes lit up.

Kenton started laughing. "All you have to do Vanessa is accept the award on behalf of Underwood Hills Winery."

"I will be proud to receive the award, Mr. Underwood."

Kenton positioned the ladder and began removing the awards from the wall.

"Why aren't you going, Mr. Underwood," Vanessa asked?

"Because I have somewhere else to go."

Vanessa felt relieved watching Kenton take down all of those dusty awards from that wall. "I commissioned my brother, Brandon to paint a Napa Valley landscape to replace these awards."

"That sounds beautiful. Mr. Underwood." Vanessa smiled.

Kenton continued to remove countless awards from the cluttered wall.

Chapter 20

Excitement filled the night air with the arrival of Henrietta's grandchildren to Poppy Hill for her birthday party. She watched as Kenton and Briana greeted each of her grandchildren as they walked through the door. After everyone had arrived, they all gathered around Henrietta in the lounge drinking cocktails and introducing their dates. Henrietta's heart was filled with happiness.

Kenton stood up and said. "I have an announcement."

Briana stood next to Kenton giving him a skeptical look.

"Briana's grand opening will be on August fifteenth, and I expect every one of you to be there."

Briana turned to Kenton and gave him a glaring look. She whispered under her breath. "Why didn't you tell them that you will be in Italy?"

Kenton whispered back. "I'll talk to you about that later tonight." He took Henrietta by the arm and walked her to the dinner table. Briana held Henrietta's other arm.

The entire Underwood clan sat around the long dining room table in front of the Napa Valley fresco. Henrietta sat at the head of the table. Kenton, Briana and Mrs. Mack sat on Henrietta's right. Her other grandchildren, Justin, Carter, Brandon, Crystal and their dates filled the remaining chairs. They all dined on crab cakes with black eyed pea sauce, Charleston red rice and fried okra.

Henrietta had mentioned to Briana that she loved chocolate.

After everyone finished dinner, Briana went into the kitchen. "We're ready Jacques."

Jacques rolled in a beautiful three layer chocolate cake filled with chocolate mousse, covered with dark chocolate frosting and dark chocolate glaze. He'd garnished the decadent cake with fudge rosettes and dark chocolate shaves.

Jacques turned out the lights and lit one candle in the middle of the cake. Everyone sang Happy Birthday to Henrietta.

It was now time to open her gifts. Henrietta watched her youngest grandson, Brandon, a successful artist, walk over to the reception desk and pull out a painting covered with a large square canvas. Brandon announced, "I want to make a toast to Granny on her eighty-fourth birthday. We are blessed to have you, Granny. You are our family's treasure."

Everyone at the table raised their glasses, saying in unison, "You are our treasure."

Brandon uncovered the painting. He revealed a portrait of Henrietta's son Joe. Everyone was pleased by the exquisite painting. "I painted this portrait of our father for you, Granny. It's my present for your birthday."

Henrietta broke out in tears when she saw the perfect image of her only child Joe looking back at her with the same sparkling eyes he'd given to Kenton, Justin, and Brandon. Carter and Crystal took after their mother's side of the family. But all of her grandchildren had Joe's smile. Wiping her eyes with her napkin, Henrietta spoke in her raspy voice. "Brandon, this painting looks just like Joe. Thank you."

Walking over to Henrietta, Brandon gave Henrietta a big hug and kiss. Kenton and Briana followed suit.

"That was so nice of you, brother." Kenton said to Brandon.

Henrietta said to all of her grandchildren. "I'm eighty four years old today, and this is the best birthday party I've ever had in my life." Everyone took turns hugging Henrietta and showering her with gifts. Minutes later, as everyone sat at the table talking over one another catching up on what was happening in their lives, Crystal gasped. All eyes faced the reservation desk. A voice spoke out. "What's she doing here?" There was a silent pause for what felt like an eternity.

Tiffany stood at the reservation desk in a dramatic pose wearing a dinner suit, heavy makeup and extra thick lip gloss all in her signature color—red. Kenton's mother Jewell had informed Tiffany that Kenton was getting married. Tiffany's only reason for coming to Henrietta's birthday party was to break up Kenton and Briana.

Briana stared at Kenton. "She's your ex. What are you going to do?"

"Excuse me everyone." Kenton walked over to Tiffany. "What are you doing here? This is a private party Tiffany. You weren't invited."

"Your mother didn't say it was a private party."

"What does my mother have to do with this?"

"She invited me." Tiffany's resentful eyes swept over Kenton. "She told me you're getting married."

Briana studied Tiffany, trying to figure her out.

"What does she want?" Crystal asked Briana.

"I'm not sure. I know Tiffany still has it bad for Kenton, but I have no idea why she crashed Henrietta's party."

"How can she still have it bad for Kenton if they broke up years ago?" Crystal whispered.

"Come on. Let's take this outside." Kenton said to Tiffany. After leading her out the front door, they talked on the front porch. "My mother had no right to invite you here Tiffany."

Briana strolled over to the reservation desk to hear their conversation. She began slowly opening and closing every drawer. She glanced over to the door, and saw they'd left it cracked open. She could hear them, but she couldn't see them. She searched through the bottom drawer, as quiet as a mouse, while she listened to their conversation.

"I don't want any of your mess, Tiffany. You need to leave now!" Kenton demanded.

Touching Kenton's face with her hand, Tiffany, gave him a longing look.

Kenton pushed her hand away from his face.

"Can't we work things out? I want you back," she said, ignoring his brushoff.

Kenton spoke through clenched teeth. "Tiffany, we've been through this a million times."

Tiffany narrowed her eyes in response to his continuous rejection. "How can you prefer that skinny toothpick of a woman over me?" she said, while calling Briana derogatory names.

Standing up straight, Briana saw red when Tiffany called her toothpick. She hated that word.

"I'm not going to stand here and let you insult Briana."

Briana smiled when she heard Kenton stand up for her.

"Come on. Let me walk you to your car." Kenton pulled by her arm.

"Stop. You're hurting me." Tiffany said. Looking into his eyes, Tiffany touched his face once again. "You know you love me."

Kenton pushed her hand away as he lessened his grip. They took a step off the porch. "You're crazy." Kenton said.

Briana eased closer to the cracked door. She saw them standing at the bottom of the porch.

The boisterousness of the family gathering muffled Kenton and Tiffany's conversation. Briana inched closer to the cracked door.

"You have to go. Now." Kenton growled.

"I will, but first I want you to know how much I've missed you Kenton."

Briana peeked through the cracked door.

Tiffany caught a glimpse of Briana's eyes. At that moment, as if on cue, Tiffany gave Kenton a sloppy kiss all over his mouth and face, leaving bright red lip gloss all over his shirt collar and face.

Briana gasped when she saw Kenton kissing Tiffany. She instinctively reacted by running upstairs. Kenton had told her that he didn't love Tiffany. But to see him kissing Tiffany like that, brought out deep feelings of insecurity in Briana.

Kenton pushed Tiffany away from him so hard that she almost fell to the ground. But in that fraction of a second, it was too late, the damage had been done. Briana had seen the kiss. "What are you doing Tiffany?" Kenton had his back to the door.

Tiffany smirked when she saw Briana run upstairs. Her face gleamed in victory. She'd accomplished what she came there to do. To break them up with a kiss. Briana took the bait. Now, let's see Kenton get out of this mess, a voice inside Tiffany's head said.

After reaching her bedroom, Briana collapsed on top of her bed feeling broken inside. Ten minutes later, for the sake of Henrietta, she managed to wipe away her uncontrollable tears and regain her composure. The last thing she wanted to do was ruin Henrietta's birthday party. With stiff strides, she walked back downstairs, holding on tightly to the stair rail. Kenton and Tiffany were still standing near the front porch when she'd reached the bottom stair. Tiffany was still trying to get him back. Briana walked through the front door, and closed it so the family wouldn't hear what she had to say.

With a broken heart, Briana looked at the red lip gloss smudged all over Kenton's collar and face. He'd undoubtedly wiped most of it off of his face and lips with the stained handkerchief he was holding. But she still saw remnants on his cheek. "How could you deceive me?" Briana asked. She held back tears of disappointment. She folded her arms, waiting for his response. "I saw the kiss."

"Briana, please let me explain." Kenton pleaded with Briana trying to find the words to explain that kiss. His body turned rigid in a defensive posture. He felt his blood pressure rising. Scrambling thoughts turned over in his mind as he searched for words to explain that unexpected kiss. He knew how it must have looked to Briana.

Like a hawk waiting for its prey to die, Tiffany waited for them to break up.

Briana eyeballed Tiffany then turned away. "Let you explain what? I saw you kiss her Kenton. How can you explain that?"

"I didn't kiss her Briana. She kissed me."

Briana held up her hand. "Stop with your semantics! I know what I saw. Clinching her hand until her nails made an imprint on her palm, Briana looked at Tiffany wearing a smirk on her face. She couldn't take another minute of this drama. "You both need to leave right now."

"Briana, baby. Listen to me." Kenton begged.

Briana held her hand up. "You need to go Kenton."

Pressing his lips together, Kenton walked into the parking lot. He couldn't think of the words to explain the kiss. Briana was too upset to hear him. Kenton got into his truck, and drove off. He knew all Briana needed to do was cool off.

Briana turned to face Tiffany. Everything Kiara taught her about standing up to bullies came back to her memory. She warned Tiffany. "You better leave while you can."

Tiffany placed her hands on her hips and stepped into Briana's space. Speaking in a low, threatening voice, she stretched out her words. "As I said before, I'm not going to let you take my man." Her top lip curled over her lip-gloss streaked teeth as she spoke. "Kenton and I have a long history together. We've known each other since middle school, and there's no way, I'm going to let some skinny woman like you come in between us."

With balled fists, Briana stood her ground, barely tolerating Tiffany's jealous threats.

Turning up her nose, and looking at Briana up and down, Tiffany spat out her hateful words. "I can't see why he's attracted to a number two pencil of a woman like you."Tiffany pushed all of Briana's hot buttons.

Briana saw red. "Get out!" She pointed to the parking lot. It took everything within Briana's power not to slap Tiffany. But Briana didn't want to be charged with assault.

Before, walking into the parking lot, Tiffany tossed her hair over her shoulders in a gesture of defiance while glaring at Briana. "Kenton was the best lover I've ever had." Her eyes were icy and cruel.

The sound of police sirens prompted Tiffany to pick up her pace. Eyeing alternative exits, she climbed into her SUV and sped away.

Briana was filled with pain and mistrust. She stood on the front porch watching Tiffany drive away in her black Escalade embellished with a solid gold personalized license plate displaying the words Sexy Diva, and twenty four inch tire rims.

After the police had arrived, Mrs. Mack rushed outside. She'd called the police when she saw Briana run upstairs. "I called the police. Is everything okay?"

"Everything is under control Miss Mack. Go back to the party." Briana told the police that everything was okay. After the police had left, Briana went back to the party. She and Mrs. Mack went into the kitchen to talk about what happened.

Briana went back to the table and announced that Kenton had gone for the evening. Everyone looked at each other.

Brandon and Crystal walked over to Henrietta and asked. "What happened, Granny?"

Henrietta said. "Stay out of it. Somebody drive me home."

At midnight, Briana sat in her window seat staring at the stars in the darkness. While gazing at her Douglas fir tree, uncontrollable tears ran down her face. She thought about Kenton's betrayal. Flashbacks of him kissing Tiffany broke her heart. She wept aloud unafraid that Mrs. Mack would hear her because her bedroom was sound proof.

Briana had turned off her cell phone, and had no desire to talk to Kenton or read his text messages. The image of that huge smudge of lip gloss all over his collar and face wouldn't leave her mind, or the pain of Tiffany's hurtful words. Hot tears began to choke her. Briana repeated in her mind for the millionth time. Kenton doesn't love her. But how could she deny what she saw with her eyes. She reasoned, if Kenton loved Tiffany before, then maybe he still had feelings for her now. Maybe he was in denial about being in love with Tiffany? Briana had worked so hard to overcome her problem with bad luck. Now her old belief would be resurrected by one kiss. How could she ever get that kiss out of her memory? Her mind was caught up in a circle of confusion. Tiffany could have Kenton. Briana was done.

Kenton lay in bed tossing and turning all night. He was angry about the events at his grandmother's birthday party. He shook his head at the memory of Tiffany sucker punching him with that sloppy kiss. How could he be so gullible to allow himself to be manipulated by Tiffany? He couldn't blame Briana for misunderstanding the kiss, because he would feel the same way if he saw Briana kissing another man. All he cared about now was coming up with the words to explain that kiss to Briana. But how could he explain something as ambiguous as an unwanted kiss? He'd already tried to explain it to Briana, but his explanation was unclear and she was too angry to hear him. Disgusted, Kenton pulled the covers over his shoulder and went to sleep.

Chapter 21

Briana sat in her office staring into space as she remembered the unimaginable events of last evening. The image of Kenton and Tiffany kissing, and that huge smudge of red lip gloss all over the side of his face and shirt collar plagued her mind. She could still hear Tiffany's cruel words and threats.

Briana wanted to find out from Kenton if he was still in love with Tiffany. Feeling betrayed by the man she loved, she woke up angry and hurt this morning, unable to find any peace. She had to find out the truth. Finally turning on her cell phone, she called Kenton. An honest answer to her question would give her some solace.

Kenton's cell phone rang as he sat behind his library desk finishing his Louis L' Amour book.

When Briana's number flashed on his cell phone, Kenton jumped up from his chair and pushed the talk button.

"Can you come over?"

"Sure. I'll be right there," he said rushing his words. Finally, she'd calmed down. Feeling relief from hearing her voice, a pang of nervousness fluttered in his gut, in his eagerness to explain what happened. Even though, he knew that looks could be deceiving, he didn't fool himself into thinking it would be easy to explain that kiss. He arrived quickly.

Briana led him into her office because she didn't want any of the staff to overhear their conversation.

Kenton tried to kiss Briana, but she turned her face away. "I have one questions for you Kenton."

Holding his breath he asked. "What's that?"

Briana lifted her chin. "Do you still love her?"

With wide, rounded eyes Kenton didn't blink, "No, I do not." He walked closer to Briana. "I never loved Tiffany. Call her crazy, jealous, or obnoxious, but her main problem is that she just can't take rejection."

"I thought you were going to get a restraining order?"

Kenton hunched his shoulders. "I haven't had a chance to go to court."

Briana frowned at Kenton, thinking about his encounter with Tiffany at Ricardo's. His procrastination in obtaining a restraining order bothered Briana. There was no sense in asking why he hadn't gone to court, because she knew he was preparing for his trip to Italy.

"Have you at least talked with her about filing a restraining order?" Briana asked.

"No, I haven't."

Kenton lowered his head. All he could do was apologize. "I'm sorry that Tiffany hurt you Briana. All I can do is apologize and ask you to forgive me and ignore Tiffany."

"Ignore Tiffany? How can I ignore that calculating, manipulative woman? It's obvious you can ignore her by putting off getting a restraining order, but I can't. What if her jealousy causes her to hurt you or me?"

"I promise. I'll get one." The thought of Tiffany hurting Briana was unbearable. With Tiffany showing up in the same places as him and Briana, Kenton was beginning to wonder if she was stalking them. Briana was right. Tiffany's actions were becoming progressively worse.

"It's too late now. Our relationship is over." Glaring at him through painful eyes, Briana said. "You said you don't love her, but your actions speak for you. You allow Tiffany to stalk us all over town without trying to stop her. I think you enjoy having her chase after you because it feeds your male ego. You could have stopped her a long time ago Kenton."

"No." Kenton held his head in the palms of his hands. How could their relationship fall apart like this? All over a misunderstood kiss and a restraining order. How could Briana think he was still in love with Tiffany? Didn't she believe anything he'd told her about his relationship with Tiffany? This misunderstanding was becoming increasingly complicated. It was clear that Briana was still angry. He stood there listening to Briana. He knew she wasn't ready to hear anything else he had to say.

Briana pulled off her engagement ring and threw it at him. "Here give this to Tiffany." She said, giving him a painful look.

Kenton couldn't believe his ears. Where was the warm, sensitive, vulnerable woman he'd met in the rundown cottage? He'd never seen this side of Briana. He didn't want their relationship to end, especially over Tiffany. He could have kicked himself for not getting that restraining order after the incident at Ricardo's. Since he didn't want to make Briana feel any more pain, he left her engagement ring on the floor where it fell and walked out of her office.

Chapter 22

The piercing sound of the fire alarm woke Briana up out of a deep sleep. Sitting up in her bed, she looked around but didn't see any smoke. Getting out of her bed, she began sniffing around her bedroom for smoke. Looking out of her bedroom window, she saw smoke rising from her Douglas fir tree. She immediately called emergency for the fire department, but they'd already received a call from the dispatcher, and were on the way. Taking another look, she saw the fire racing up the tree. Without a second thought for her safety, she rushed downstairs, ran out the back door and turned on the garden hose. While spraying her beloved Christmas tree, a look of despair spread across her face as she watched the fire crawl up the tree. She said a little prayer as she fixated on the burning tree that symbolized her mother's love. After unsuccessfully extinguishing the fire, she stood back with hot tears rolling down her cheeks and watched the tree turn into a soaring inferno.

Although the fire department had arrived within five minutes, too much damage had happened to the tree by the time they'd arrived. A strapping firefighter ordered Briana to step away for her safety. Briana stepped back, falling to her knees as she watched her tree burn in flames.

Henrietta woke up when she heard the fire engines. Pushing herself out of bed, and grabbing her cane, she walked over to her window and saw flashing fire engine lights pass her house. They stopped at Briana's restaurant. Looking up into the black sky, she cringed when she saw glowing red flames. "Oh, my God! What's happened?" She immediately picked up the phone and called Briana. No one answered. She speed dialed Kenton's number.

Kenton answered the phone.

"Briana's restaurant is on fire."

"What!" Kenton sat up in his bed. Distressing thoughts crossed his mind.

"I tried to call Briana, but she's not answering," Henrietta said hysterically.

In one swift motion, Kenton slipped into his jeans and ran out of the house still wearing his pajama top and slippers. Jumping into his truck, he gripped the steering wheel and sped like a speed demon over to Poppy Hill. Briana's safety was all that mattered to him. Halfway there, he braced himself, because he didn't know what he would find.

Kenton drove into the driveway and saw a blackened skeleton of Briana's Douglas fir tree still smoking. He stopped a firefighter walking around the building looking for hot spots.

"My fiancé is in there. Is she all right?"

"There were no casualties. We've contained the fire with minimal damage to the structure. The owner of the property is inside."

Kenton exhaled as he watched the fire trucks leave. He wiped his forehead as he walked up the front steps and tried to open the door. Briana had locked the door. He called Briana on his cell phone, but she wouldn't answer. He banged on her door while calling out her name. She still wouldn't answer. He texted her. "Are you hurt?"

Briana returned his text message. "No. I'm fine. I don't want to see you because I'm still angry."

Kenton felt relieved to read Briana's text. All that mattered to Kenton, was that she wasn't hurt. He got back into his truck and drove back home.

The next morning, smoke still lingered in Briana's bedroom when she woke up. She smelled a toxic mixture of wood siding and paint mainly. There was also an underlying stench of burnt pine permeating through her bedroom window. Feeling groggy from a sleepless night, she sat on the side of her bed. She leaned forward, laying her head on her arms. Nightmares of her restaurant burning down had haunted her all night long. She worried if the fire would prevent her from staying on schedule with her grand opening. Closing her eyes, she whispered a little prayer. She wanted the strength to overcome this setback. She lifted her head from her arms. She got out of bed and moved around with downturned features. Walking over to her window seat, she looked up at the blackened skeleton branches of her once beautiful tree. Gazing into the azure sky, she believed her mother would want her to stay on track with her grand opening. She sat there counting her blessings. Briana gave thanks, beginning with her life. Things could have turned out worse. She could have died in the fire, and her restaurant could have burned down to the ground.

Thank goodness, she'd taken Rex's advice and installed a state of the art, smoke detector and sprinklers. She'd installed them on the outside and the inside of the restaurant, when she had it built. As a result of her decision, there was little damage to the building. Several hours later, she called Rex asking him if he could come over, to take a look at the damages.

Later that afternoon, after inspecting her restaurant, Rex said he could probably make the repairs in a week or so, just in time for her grand opening. Briana was not going to let the fire or the loss of her tree, ruin her grand opening. After ending her conversation with Rex, she showered, dressed and went to work.

Nathaniel Young was handcuffed, in his office, by a burly Federal Police Officer. Other police officers escorted customers out of Edibles restaurant in the middle of the day. Lights flashed as photographers took photos. Camera men recorded footage of the event. A news reporter spoke into a microphone announcing that Nathaniel Young, owner of Edibles restaurant, was being arrested for Tax evasion.

Nathaniel's thoughts were on his daughter Tiffany as he walked down the hall in handcuffs. He now saw clearly, how he'd ruined her life by controlling her finances, and forcing her to depend on him for everything. Who would take care of her now? She would no longer have an income, now that the IRS had frozen his assets. He'd, fortunately, stashed away emergency cash in a safe deposit box in Tiffany's name at a local bank. He'd told her about the safe deposit box shortly before the police arrived. He told her not to come to the restaurant today.

Nathaniel spoke to the camera as the officer escorted him toward the police car. "My lawyer will get me out before it gets dark." Nathaniel barked out, speaking to the cameras. "I'm telling you I did nothing wrong."

The police officer placed his hand on Nathaniel's head, while pushing him inside the police car.

Chapter 23

Henrietta hadn't seen Briana since her birthday party. She'd talked to Briana after the fire, but she missed having Briana over for Sunday dinner. Henrietta watched Kenton staring into his plate at the dinner table. She wanted to know what was going on with him and Briana. She was tired of watching Kenton mope around the house running into this and dropping that.

"Baby boy, what's going on with you and Briana?" She hadn't meddled in Kenton's love life with Briana until now. Henrietta overheard Kenton begging Briana on the phone one day. She thought that they'd had a lover's quarrel over Tiffany the night of the party. Henrietta had no idea that Kenton and Briana had broken up.

"We broke up Granny." Kenton felt despondent and decided to open up to the only woman in this world he trusted more than Briana.

"You know what you have to do. You have to go over there and talk to her." Henrietta said.

"She won't see me or answer my calls Granny," he admitted. Being separated from Briana, caused him to suffer from insomnia. He hadn't slept in days. He missed Briana and would do anything to get her back. He felt too embarrassed to tell Henrietta that he'd already tried to go there many times. He'd even tried to call her over seventy-five times, but she wouldn't take any of his calls or see him.

With a heavy sigh, Henrietta recalled the only time she'd ever left her husband Frank. "Let me tell you a story Kenton," Henrietta said, lifting a fork full of unseasoned peas into her mouth. "When your grandfather and I were young, I tried to leave him." She paused. "Yes, I did." Staring into Kenton's eyes, she said. "To this day, I can't remember what we were fighting about." Adjusting her napkin under her neck, she continued. "I left Frank and went back home to my daddy. Your grandfather came over to my daddy's house and had a little talk with daddy. Since your grandfather hadn't mistreated me, daddy said he could take me back home. Your grandfather politely took me by the hand and brought me back home. It was as simple as that. All I remember is we made up, and I never left Frank again."

Late that night, Kenton thought about his grandfather Frank. Maybe he would go over to Poppy Hill and take Briana back to Sage Creek. None of this would have happened if it weren't for Tiffany. He became angry when he recalled how Tiffany had sucker punched him with that kiss in front of Briana. He should have called the police when Tiffany first showed her face. Better yet, he should have filed a restraining order, like Briana advised. He knew trouble was following Tiffany the moment she walked through that door. He had to find a way to prove to Briana that Tiffany set him up. He knew Tiffany would never admit to her deceitful act, but maybe she would tell the truth for a price. He was desperate and would do anything to get Briana back.

Tiffany had watched the Federal Police Officers take her father away in handcuffs on television. She knew her father meant well, but for years she felt oppressed under his authoritative, controlling ways. Without a doubt, she loved her father, but when she watched him get into that police car, she felt as if a ton of bricks had been lifted from her shoulders. In those two weeks, she prayed for the first time in her life and transformed into a new person. She felt as light as a feather. Malicious thoughts or a desire for revenge no longer ruled her mind. She finally felt at peace with herself.

Tiffany knew her father had used his money and power to control her. She lived lavishly and irresponsibly at his expense. She received a healthy monthly allowance to pay her credit cards and bills. All she had to do was ask, and her father would bail her out of any financial disasters she'd created.

Tiffany watched the Feds seize all of the restaurant equipment, and put it in storage. She knew that Nathaniel's files and office furniture were next. A knock on the front door brought Tiffany back to the present.

Tiffany answered the door. It was Kenton.

"Can I come in?"

"Sure come in."

Kenton followed Tiffany through the empty restaurant into Nathaniel's office.

"I'm cleaning out daddy's office," Tiffany said as she began placing desk accessories, photos and office supplies into a box. Before her world fell apart, she would have done anything to get Kenton back. Now she focused inwardly, something she'd never done before. All of her life she'd never looked inward to solve her problems. But after her father's arrest, she'd grown up. She was no longer daddy's little girl. Now she had to stand on her own two feet.

After her transformation, she'd come to realize that her unrealistic pursuit of Kenton was childish. By looking inside of herself, she began to feel ashamed of some of the terrible things she'd said and done. Looking at Kenton standing in front of her father's desk, Tiffany felt compelled to apologize for her dastardly deeds. "I was..." She stammered. "I mean, you and Briana didn't deserve how I treated you."

"Are you trying to apologize for what you did?" Kenton took a step back.

"Yes." She lowered her gaze.

"Are you okay, Tiffany? You seem...different."

"I am different." She confessed. She opened up like a blooming flower to Kenton. "My father's arrest has changed me in a good way."

"How's that?"

"When I saw my father get into that police car, I got on my knees and prayed for the first time in my life." She paused. "When I got up, I felt like a new person. My attitude and my focus on life changed."

"Good for you Tiffany."

"I realized that I no longer have my father to depend on." She paused. "Now, I have to depend on myself for everything. I have to take life seriously." She realized that her selfishness, vanity and narcissistic attitude that once ruled her behavior, were now unimportant.

"Sometimes, people have to reach rock bottom before they can change. Remember when I told you that your desire to hurt people would backfire?"

Tiffany nodded her head. "I remember."

"I warned you that you were walking down the wrong path."

"Yes you did," Tiffany remembered.

"I guess my words didn't fall on deaf ears."

"No Kenton. I heard your words loud and clear. I thank you for them. I just hope you can accept my apology for treating you and Briana so badly."

"I accept your apology Tiffany. But now, I need your help."

"Anything," she said putting a calendar into the box.

"Will you tell Briana the truth about that kiss?"

Even though, Kenton knew bribery was a terrible idea, he'd come prepared to pay Tiffany to tell Briana the truth about the kiss. He hadn't been able to eat or sleep for the past two weeks. He missed Briana more than ever. The constant tightness in his chest had made him begin to wonder if his heart was giving out. He would do anything to get Briana back. Fortunately due to Tiffany's change of heart, he wouldn't need to resort to bribery.

"Yes. I'll tell Briana the truth." Tiffany nodded her head in the affirmative. "I have something else to tell you," she said putting an ashtray into the box.

"What else?" Kenton asked.

"I set Briana's restaurant on fire."

"No." Kenton moaned.

"Yes. I'm sorry."

"You could have killed her!" His eyes glared angrily. "You better be glad nothing happened to her. I would have never forgiven you." He paused for a second. "I only want to get Briana back. I can't think about your heinous act right now."

"Should I tell Briana?"

"No! It would be like opening Pandora's Box right now. Don't mention that to Briana. There's nothing you can do about that now. Just tell her the truth about that kiss. That's the only way I can get her back."

"I feel better now that I've come clean with the truth," Tiffany confessed.

"So what are you going to do now?" Kenton crossed his arms.

"I'm leaving town."

"Where are you going?"

"Southern California."

"What are you going to do in Southern California?"

"Start over." She raised her shoulders. "Maybe, I'll find a job in the travel industry or become an interior decorator."

"I can see you supporting yourself in any of those fields. What are you going to do for money until you get a job? I heard the Feds seized your dad's bank accounts."

"I have enough money to last until I get a job. Daddy said he'll never be able to run a successful business in Napa again. He's the one who told me to move to Southern California." With a long low sigh, she asked. "So when do you want me to tell Briana the truth?"

"We can ride over there right now and tell her."

"Give me a chance to clean up. I'll be ready in a minute."

Kenton nodded and sat down.

Thirty minutes later, Kenton drove Tiffany over to Poppy Hill.

"Sit tight. I'll bring Briana out." Kenton said. "After you tell her the truth, call a taxi and leave. Can you do that?"

"I can do that." Tiffany sat in the truck quietly waiting.

Kenton walked up the steps and stood on the porch. He paused for a moment to collect himself. He opened the door and was met by Trevor. To protect Briana, Trevor blocked Kenton from coming closer. Briana stood behind the reservation desk. Kenton gave Trevor a hard look, but Trevor didn't move.

"You can leave us alone Trevor." Briana said.

"I'll be in the kitchen if you need me," Trevor said as he left.

"What are you doing here?" Briana asked in a serious voice.

"I came to talk to you Briana. We have to talk," Kenton said.

"Let's go into my office." Kenton followed Briana into her office and sat in the lime green chair. Briana sat behind her desk.

"First of all Briana," he rubbed the back of his neck. "I... We've been separated for more than a month." He closed his eyes. "I need to clear up a few misunderstandings before-" Finding himself tongue-tied over his burning love for Briana, Kenton tried to concentrate on what he wanted to say.

"I'm all ears." Briana had cooled down. She listened to Kenton's sexy voice and observed his handsome face. She thought about how much she'd missed him.

"First and foremost, please hear me out. I did not kiss Tiffany. She kissed me. In fact, she staged that kiss hoping you would see it. And, I do not love Tiffany." He emphasized his words again. "Tiffany is willing to admit that she staged that kiss."

Briana gave Kenton a surprised look. "What?"

"Yes. She's outside, right now, ready to admit the truth."

"Where outside?" Briana stood up to look through the window and saw Tiffany leaning against Kenton's truck.

"Come on let's go." Kenton took Briana by her hand and walked out to his truck where Tiffany was standing.

Briana walked with Kenton into the parking lot. Briana's eyes locked with Tiffany's.

Tiffany lowered her head. When Briana came closer, Tiffany looked directly into Briana's eyes and came clean. "Briana, I staged that kiss the night of the party. Kenton wasn't kissing me. I was kissing him. Kenton pushed me away. But, you didn't see that. You only saw what I wanted you to see. I saw you peeking through the door, and I watched you run upstairs." Tiffany paused for a moment. "I am so sorry for what I did."

Briana blinked her eyes. Am I in the Twilight Zone? Did I just hear Tiffany apologize? Briana thought to herself. "What happened to make you want to apologize?" Briana asked. She didn't dare trust the words coming from Tiffany's mouth.

"It's a long story," Tiffany said. "All I can say is that I'm sorry for doing so many mean spirited things to hurt you and Kenton."

Briana stood there with a dumbfounded look on her face. She turned to face Kenton.

Kenton read Briana's mind. "I'll explain it to you," Kenton said.

"It's obvious that Kenton loves you," Tiffany continued. "He's a good man."

Briana couldn't believe her ears. Tiffany had made an about face in her attitude.

"Again, I'm sorry Briana." Tiffany quickly pulled out her cell phone from her handbag and called a taxi.

"Come on Briana. Let's go back inside." Kenton took Briana's hand.

Content with Tiffany's confession, Briana, looked up at Kenton and smiled.

They walked back toward Briana's office leaving Tiffany talking on her cell phone.

Kenton gave Briana a detailed explanation of Tiffany's change of heart as they walked into the restaurant. Kenton turned his head around and silently formed the words, thank you, with his lips. Tiffany waved her hand.

Kenton and Briana reached Briana's office and sat down. "I never got a chance to tell you at Granny's party that I'm not going to Italy to receive that award," Kenton said.

"Huh?" Briana touched her parted lips with her fingers. "But I thought you wanted to go?"

Kenton looked deeply into Briana's eyes and spoke from his heart. Reaching across her desk, he took Briana's hand into his caressing it softly. "I decided it's more important for me to support you at your grand opening instead of going to Italy to accept another award. I thought about the possibility of losing you Briana." He kissed her hand. "And I just couldn't take the risk." He held both of her hands. "Having you in my life is more important to me than anything in the world. I wish I would have never fought with you over Italy. Forgive me?"

"Yes. I forgive you Kenton." Her heart began to soften, and her eyes began to glisten as she listened to this wonderful man. Kenton was the man who'd helped her with her building permit. He was always there when she needed him the most. He was the man who pulled her out of a dark pit of believing she had bad luck when it came to love. He was the man who encouraged her to reach out to her extended family.

A smile began to build on Briana's face. Looking up at Kenton through long lashes, she turned around to open her file cabinet. She pulled a decorative box. She opened it and pulled out her engagement ring. She sat the ring on her desk while looking up at Kenton through seductive eyes.

Kenton remembered her throwing the ring on the floor. "All I want is you Briana, nothing else."

Briana couldn't believe how gullible she'd been listening to Tiffany. Kenton tried to tell her about the kiss the night of the party, but she was too hurt to hear his words. How could she ever forgive herself? "I'm sorry Kenton for not listening to you. I was wrong."

Kenton reached for her hand. "I love you Briana, and Granny loves you. We both want you to be a part of our family. There are so many things I love about you Briana. I love your Low Country cooking; I love your sweet southern accent; I love your hard-headed independent spirit, and I love the way you challenge me. You are my best friend, Briana. I love that I can tell you things I've never told anyone else. I need to have you in my life, as much as I need air to breathe, and you are coming home with me to Sage Creek right now."

He remembered the story about his grandfather grasping his grandmother's hand and taking her back home. Taking Briana's hand, he said. "Come on baby let's go." Kenton saw her ring lying on her desk. Picking it up, he said. "Here, put this back on." He slid the ring back on her finger.

They walked toward Kenton's truck. "Are we good?" Kenton asked.

Briana smiled. "Yeah, we're good."

"I have a surprise for you," Kenton said as he opened the car door.

"I love surprises," Briana said giving him a curious look.

"Yesterday, I bought a six foot, Douglas fir tree. I'm going to plant it outside of your kitchen window in the morning."

"Tears of joy streamed down Briana's face. Thank you." She sat close to Kenton in the truck, leaning her head on his shoulder.

They drove to Sage Creek and made love all night.

Henrietta sat at the dinner table with Kenton and Briana. "I have a confession to make."

Briana braced herself as she listened to Henrietta. She'd heard enough confessions to last a lifetime.

"Your grandmother Lillie and I made a promise to each other when we were young mothers. We both grew up without sisters. We both wanted to become sisters through marriage." Opening up a small locket, she wore around her neck, she asked Briana to read it.

Briana walked over to Henrietta and took the locket. One side read sisters. The other side read forever. "Sisters Forever," Briana said. She walked back to her chair and stared at Henrietta. "What does it mean?"

"Your grandmother asked me to look after you in case anything ever happened to her. She wanted you to renovate that cottage and marry one of my grandsons. She and I wanted that because we raised our children with the same values. This locket represents our hope that our dream of being sisters would one day come true. I only wish that Lillie could be here to see you and Kenton." Henrietta opened her arms. "Come and give me a hug granddaughter."

The next morning, Kenton and Briana drove up to Atlas Peak to check on the vines. Kenton held Briana's hand while they walked through the vineyard. The only sound they heard that early in the morning were loud blue Scrub Jays and black birds. Kenton loved the country life. A place where he could hear himself think. He was glad that he had a woman who felt the same way. "I'm going to produce the best Chardonnay, Sauvignon Blanc, and Riesling wines our customers have ever tasted." Gathering Briana into his arms in the middle of his vineyard, Kenton held her snugly kissing her slow and thoughtful. "I am the happiest man in the world."

Chapter 24

Briana's grand opening had finally arrived. Nightfall had darkened the sky, and electricity ran its current through the atmosphere. She'd hired an event planner to erect a large tent pitched in back of the restaurant with views of the Poppy field that glistened in the darkness. Seating for over three hundred people had been set up, most of them friends, family, business owners, and food critics. The event planner provided tables, chairs, flowers, bartenders, servers, chefs, and cooks. Briana and her staff planned to oversee the menu items offered to the food critics who all sat at the same table.

Briana saw the Michelin food critic enter. The Michelin Red Guide was the oldest and best-known hotel and restaurant guide that awarded the Michelin stars. One star indicated very good cuisine in its category. A two-star ranking represented excellent cuisine, worth a detour, and a rare three stars represented restaurants offering exceptional cuisine, worth a special journey. Briana wanted to get three stars. Stopping for a moment, Briana examined her desire to win three stars, and now understood how Kenton must have felt winning all of those wine awards. She could see how the anticipation of winning an award could become addicting. She hated hypocrites and now she felt like one. She made a mental note to apologize to Kenton.

Making one last round in the kitchen, Briana saw that Jacques and the staff had everything under control. She focused on her role as mistress of ceremonies. She closed her eyes, said a little prayer and prepared to go to the podium to welcome everyone. Looking like a goddess, Briana wore an elegant ivory Dior column gown and wore her hair in an up hairstyle. She kept her jewelry to a minimum.

After everyone had taken their seats, Briana picked up the microphone to introduce herself. She showed no fear or angst only graceful poise. "Good evening. I'm Briana Rutledge, owner of Poppy Hill Restaurant. The name comes from a beautiful field of orange poppies growing in the back of the restaurant." She continued with her speech giving her grandmother Lillie, Henrietta and Kenton special recognition. "I would not be standing here today if it had not been for my grandmother and the Underwood family. They all supported my dream of opening Poppy Hill."

"I had a vision to introduce Low Country cuisine to the Napa Valley." She gave her audience the definition. "Low Country is the name of the cuisine that I serve. It originated in an area located between Savannah, Georgia, and the South Carolina coastline. The cuisine is similar to West Indian, Cajun and Creole cooking."

Looking around the audience, her eyes locked onto Kenton's. A faint smile crossed her face. Warmth radiated through her body as she looked lovingly into his eyes. "I want to take this time to thank my fiancé Kenton Underwood and his grandmother Mrs. Henrietta Underwood." Her eyes never left Kenton's. "Kenton, please come up."

Kenton smiled and waved at the audience as he walked up to the podium. "Hello Napa. You all know me. Let me introduce you to the next member of the Underwood family. Briana Rutledge is the woman I'm going to marry. How do you like her?" The audience began clapping. Kenton kissed and hugged Briana in front of everyone.

Taking the microphone, Briana announced. "Dinner is served. Enjoy!"

They walked back to their table hand in hand.

When they reached their table, Briana confessed. "I've been a hypocrite Kenton. I wanted to win three stars from the Michelin food critic more than anything. Now I understand how you feel about winning all those awards. Please forgive me for being so hard on you."

"Don't worry about that, green eyes. Let's just enjoy the evening."

Briana and Kenton sat close to each other at the table. "I'm so in love with you Kenton," Briana said.

"I love you back baby."

Henrietta wiped her cataract eyes with her napkin after watching their show of affection.

Briana nudged Kenton. "There's the Michelin food critic over there."

Kenton pushed himself up from his chair. "Excuse me baby, I'll be right back." He walked over to the Michelin food critic who he'd heard was French. "Welcoming to Poppy Hill Restaurant," Kenton said in fluent French.

Briana listened as a quartet played contemporary music with a female vocalist. Briana saw the critic taste her Low Country Boil and mustard greens. Briana looked around the room when the critic began eating. Briana listened as the whole room became quiet as they watched her reaction. Briana held her breath as the critic closed her eyes, tasting a fork full of mustard greens. Briana watched her face closely because she knew the greens were melting in her mouth. The critic opened her eyes and gave Briana a wink. Smiling, Briana knew that the rest of her evening would be a success.

Kenton joined Briana at the table.

Briana grinned. "Everything is going well tonight Kenton. I've already received several large private party requests."

"That's great," Kenton said.

Briana felt giddy as every food critic and Napa business owners came up to her to put in reservations for their parties. They all thanked her for bringing her special style of cuisine to the Napa Valley. "I can't wait to read the local reviews tomorrow," Briana said to Kenton.

Later that night, Briana saw that Kenton had fallen asleep. Running her fingers through his soft chest hair, she whispered in his ear, "I love you."

On a warm spring afternoon the following spring, Kenton and Briana were married in Briana's gazebo in the middle of her poppy field. The wedding planner had transformed the winery into an elegant space for the reception. Poppy Hill catered the event.

"I'm glad Briana asked me to be her matron of honor," Kiara said, riding in a golf cart next to Mrs. Mack. They were both dressed in a pale peach organza dresses.

"I'm honored to walk her down the aisle," Mrs. Mack said.

Henrietta followed in a golf cart behind them. She was now confined to a wheel chair.

Kenton and his second brother Justin, the family attorney, stood with the minister inside the Gazebo wearing black tuxedos with pale peach accessories.

After arriving on a golf cart, Carter and Brandon helped Henrietta out of the cart into her wheelchair.

A chamber quartet in front of the gazebo began to play the wedding march. Everyone in the audience stood up to watch the matron of honor walk on the white carpet down the aisle. After Kiara walked down the aisle. Briana, escorted by Mrs. Mack, walked down the aisle.

Briana wore a white organza veil over her face. She wore a fluffy white organza shoulder-less gown and carried a bouquet of white lilies tied with poppy hued ribbon.

"You look beautiful," Kenton whispered to Briana.

"Thank you."

Holding hands, they exchanged the age-old vow

Henrietta sat in her wheelchair thinking about her promise to Lillie. She rubbed her locket and whispered under her breath. "See Lillie, we are sisters forever."

After saying their vows. Kenton removed the veil and kissed his bride Briana.

Ushers drove golf carts filled with those who couldn't walk to the Underwood Hills reception hall. Everyone dined on a Low Country meal and a five tier wedding cake made by Jacques. Briana and Kenton danced the night away and sipped champagne in

Kenton's vineyard under the stars. Briana and Kenton spent their honeymoon in Rome, Italy.

For more information about some African American wineries in Napa Valley and the State of California, please visit the Association of African American Vintners www.aaavintners.org.

Bates Creek, Napa Valley, CA now Black Coyote – Dr. Ernest Bates founder.

Brown Estate Vineyards, Napa Valley, CA – Bassett Brown.

Vision Cellars, Sonoma County, CA – E.G. "Mac" McDonald.

Rideau Vineyards, Santa Ynez Valley, CA – Iris Rideau.

Esterlina Vineyards and Winery, Anderson Valley, CA - the Sterling family.

Sharp Cellars, Sonoma, CA - Vance Sharp.

Running Tigers Wine – Daniel Bryant.

Theopolis Vineyards, Mendocino County – Theodora Lee.

About The Author

Janice L. Dennie began her writing career in 1997 with her debut novel, *The Lion of Judah*. Her second book, *Moon Goddess Queen of Sheba*, was published in August 1999. *Kenton's Vintage Affair*, book 1 in *The Underwood's of Napa Valley* series, introduces the reader to the fictitious Underwood family, owners of a successful winery in Napa Valley.

Janice was born in Denver, Colorado and raised in Northern California. After graduating from college, Janice began working for a federal agency. She services her community through various charities and non-profits. Currently, she writes full-time and lives in Northern California with her family. Janice regularly posts comments on her janicedennieauthor, Facebook page, and Twitter @jdennieauthor. She'd love to hear from you, and will reply to any email sent to her at janicedennie1@gmail.com.

To read more about Janice, visit her website at:

http://www.janicedennie.com.

Quick Order Form

Please send the following books. I understand that I may return any of them for a full refund—for any reason, no questions asked.

	QTY	PRICE	AMOUNT
KENTON'S VINTAGE AFFAIR	____	$10.00	$_____
JUSTIN'S BODY OF WORK	____	$10.00	$_____
CARTER'S HEART CONDITION	____	$10.00	$_____
THE LION OF JUDAH	____	$10.00	$_____
	Sales Tax & Postage		$_____
	Total		$_____

(Please add $3.00 per book for California Sales Tax and Postage.)

Name:_____

Address:_____

City:_____ State:____ Zip:_____

Email:_____

My Check ____ Money Order____ is enclosed. Please allow up to six weeks for delivery.

____Visa ____ MasterCard ____ Discover

Card number:_____

Name on card:_____ Exp. Date:___/___
                                              MM/YY

Send completed form to:
KENTE PUBLICATIONS
P.O. Box 184
Jackson, CA 95642

Quick Order Form

Please send the following books. I understand that I may return any of them for a full refund—for any reason, no questions asked.

	QTY	PRICE	AMOUNT
KENTON'S VINTAGE AFFAIR	_____	$10.00	$_____
JUSTIN'S BODY OF WORK	_____	$10.00	$_____
CARTER'S HEART CONDITION	_____	$10.00	$_____
THE LION OF JUDAH	_____	$10.00	$_____
	Sales Tax & Postage		$_____
	Total		$_____

(Please add $3.00 per book for California Sales Tax and Postage.)

Name:_____

Address:_____

City:_____ State:____ Zip:_____

Email:_____

My Check _____ Money Order_____ is enclosed. Please allow up to six weeks for delivery.

_____Visa _____ MasterCard _____ Discover

Card number:_____

Name on card:_____Exp. Date:____/____
                                                    MM/YY

Send completed form to:
Kente Publications
P.O. Box 184
Jackson, CA 95642